THE ISOLATOR
realization of absolute solitude

Sect.002
The Igniter

REKI KAWAHARA
ILLUSTRATION BY SHIMEJI
CHARACTER DESIGN BY BEE-PEE

"I'VE GOT IT! FROM NOW ON, YOU WILL BE CALLED MIKKUN!!"

YEAR 4-CLASS 2
RIRI ISA

>> **RIRI ISA**

A MEMBER OF THE SFD, WHICH IS MADE UP OF THOSE WHO FIGHT TO PROTECT HUMANITY FROM THE RUBY EYES. HER OFFICIAL TITLE IS DIVISION CHIEF AND STRATEGIC COMMANDER OF THE MINISTRY OF HEALTH, LABOR, AND WELFARE'S INDUSTRIAL SAFETY AND HEALTH DEPARTMENT, SPECIALIZED FORCES DIVISION. SHE IS ALSO CURRENTLY A FOURTH-YEAR ELEMENTARY SCHOOL STUDENT.

"SORRY 'BOUT THAT, UTSUGI. WHAT WAS YOUR CODE NAME AGAIN...? 'ISOLATOR'? ANYWAY, WE'LL HAVE TO HAVE FUN LEVELING UP SOME OTHER TIME."

≫ **OLIVIER SAITO**
A MEMBER OF THE SFD. APPARENTLY HALF-FRENCH, HE IS A YOUNG MAN WITH A PRETTY FACE. HE TENDS TO COME AND GO AS HE PLEASES, SPENDING MOST OF HIS ON-BASE TIME PLAYING VIDEO GAMES.

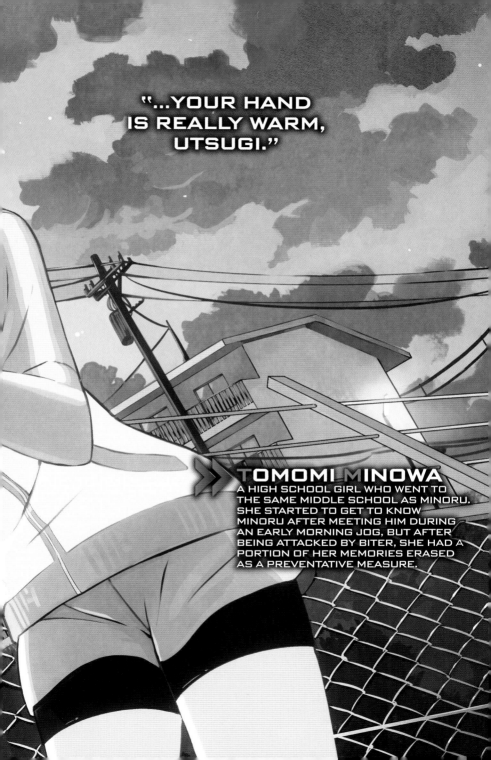

"...YOUR HAND IS REALLY WARM, UTSUGI."

TOMOMI MINOWA
A HIGH SCHOOL GIRL WHO WENT TO THE SAME MIDDLE SCHOOL AS MINORU. SHE STARTED TO GET TO KNOW MINORU AFTER MEETING HIM DURING AN EARLY MORNING JOG, BUT AFTER BEING ATTACKED BY BITER, SHE HAD A PORTION OF HER MEMORIES ERASED AS A PREVENTATIVE MEASURE.

"...!"

≫ MINORU UTSUGI

AN ORDINARY YOUNG MAN WHO LIVES
WITH HIS RELATIVE AND OLDER-SISTER
FIGURE, NORIE. HE LOVES SOLITUDE
AND HATES HAVING HIS EXISTENCE LEFT
IN THE MEMORIES OF OTHER PEOPLE.
AFTER ENCOUNTERING A MYSTERIOUS
SPHERICAL OBJECT FROM OUTER
SPACE, A THIRD EYE, A UNIQUE POWER
AWAKENS WITHIN HIM.

"EVEN SO,
I'LL BELIEVE IN
YOU."

YUMIKO AZU
A MEMBER OF THE SFD, WHICH
SPECIALIZES IN INTERCEPTING
THIRD EYE HOSTS DETERMINED
TO POSE A THREAT. SHE LEAPED
BETWEEN MINORU AND BITER WHEN
THEY FIRST FOUGHT.

"HERE, MII! SAY 'AHH...'"

>> NORIE YOSHIMIZU
AFTER BOTH OF MINORU'S PARENTS
PASSED AWAY, SHE WAS THE ONE
WHO TOOK HIM IN. WITH A BRIGHT
AND POSITIVE PERSONALITY, SHE
IS ALWAYS WORRYING ABOUT HOW
MINORU IS DOING.

THE ISOLATOR
realization of absolute solitude   CONTENTS

realization of absolute solitude

Sect.002 The Igniter

"I'M LOOKING FOR ABSOLUTE SOLITUDE... THAT'S WHY MY CODE NAME IS ISOLATOR."

REKI KAWAHARA
ILLUSTRATIONS BY SHIMEJI
CHARACTER DESIGN BY BEE-PEE

YEN
ON
NEW YORK

THE ISOLATOR Volume 2
© REKI KAWAHARA

Translation by ZephyrRz

ZETTAI NARU ISOLATOR
© REKI KAWAHARA 2015
All rights reserved.
Edited by ASCII MEDIA WORKS
First published in Japan in 2015 by KADOKAWA CORPORATION, Tokyo.
English translation rights arranged with KADOKAWA CORPORATION, Tokyo,
through Tuttle-Mori Agency, Inc., Tokyo.

English translation © 2016 by Hachette Book Group, Inc.

Yen On
Hachette Book Group
1290 Avenue of the Americas
New York, NY 10104
www.hachettebookgroup.com
www.yenpress.com

Yen On is an imprint of Hachette Book Group, Inc.
The Yen On name and logo are trademarks of Hachette Book Group, Inc.

First Yen On edition: January 2016

Library of Congress Cataloging-in-Publication Data

Names: Kawahara, Reki, author. | Shimeji, illustrator. | ZephyrRz, translator.
Title: The Isolator, realization of absolute solitude. Sect.002, The Igniter
 / Reki Kawahara ; illustrations by Shimeji ; character design by Bee-Pee ;
 translation by ZephyrRz .
Other titles: Zettai naru Isolator. English | Realization of absolute solitude.
 Sect.002, The igniter | Sect.002 The igniter | Igniter
Description: First Yen On edition. | New York : Yen On, 2016.
Identifiers: LCCN 2015034584 | ISBN 9780316268899 (hardback)
Subjects: | CYAC: Orphans—Fiction. | Solitude—Fiction. | Science fiction. |
 BISAC: FICTION / Science Fiction / Adventure.
Classification: LCC PZ7.K1755 It 2016 | DDC [Fic]—dc23 LC record available at
 http://lccn.loc.gov/2015034584

10 9 8 7 6 5 4 3 2 1

RRD-C

Printed in the United States of America

Sect. 002
THE IGNITER

1

What is a flame?

What happens when an object combusts?

In order to explain what happens during combustion, chemists in medieval Europe hypothesized an element they called "phlogiston." It was thought all combustible material contained phlogiston, and when that material was heated, it would release the phlogiston in the form of fire and smoke. However, that hypothesis was discredited after experiments showed that when a material combusts, what is left over is slightly heavier than what was there before.

Of course, now we know that combustion is a form of oxidation. Fire is the result of when heated materials mix with the air to form a flammable gas and oxidize in a chain reaction, releasing light and heat. In other words, oxygen is the key to the mystery that allows the beautiful and intense phenomenon of combustion to take place.

Oxygen.

O-x-y-g-e-n, oxygen.

"*Oxy...gen!* ♪" sang a man, who goes by the name Ayato Suka, before spreading his arms wide and taking a deep breath.

The oxygen particles from the air that were sucked in through Suka's nostrils flowed down his bronchial tubes and into his lungs, where they then passed through his alveolar sacs and into his bloodstream. The murky blood from his veins was cleansed and regained its brilliance and beautiful red color before being sent off to the rest of his body.

At the same time, tears gently flowed from under Suka's closed eyes, tears of gratitude. The intensity of his gratitude sent shivers down his spine, and goose bumps rose all over his skin.

Right now, in the mitochondria throughout Suka's body,

ATP was being synthesized through reactions with hydrogen and oxygen. This, too, was a form of combustion. Oxygen, in all its glory and with its infinite mercy, allows not just mankind, but all life, a peaceful and harmless form of combustion.

It is for that reason, we must give our greatest thanks with every breath.

But even so...*you people never...*

Suka opened his eyes and looked down at the scene below him.

He was standing on a small ledge, beyond the fence on the roof of a fifteen-story building, so the people walking on the street below looked like specks. On the road in front of the west entrance to Ikebukuro Station were long lines of taxis and private vehicles, and the wide walkways were filled with pedestrians.

Inside of the engines of the cars crawling along the congested road, oxygen was sucked into the cylinders to be mixed with aerosol gasoline and forced into performing a meaningless combustion. The ugly chorus of exhaust sounded as if the oxygen particles were screaming out in anger.

Not only that, but the oxygen breathed in by the people walking down below was also being wasted for stupid reasons. To supply the energy for their meaningless conversations and their meaningless movements, oxygen was being polluted and released as exhaust.

But even so, they never give thanks... They don't even think about the process at all.

You don't know. You don't know how glorious, how terrifying, how dangerous oxygen is.

"So I will show you," Suka sang.

The center of Suka's right palm throbbed with heat, as if it were agreeing with him, supporting him, egging him on. Suka extended his right hand, curling his fingers as if he were gripping a clear ball about ten centimeters in diameter. He had never successfully tried gripping something of this size before, but this time would be different. In preparation for this moment he had spent a month camping in the mountains of Okutama, at harmony with its sweet and fresh oxygen.

Moving his fingers, Suka focused on one of the people on the walkway far below.

It was a young businessman wearing a gray suit. Perhaps he was waiting for someone, as he had stood on the edge of the walkway for about thirty minutes without moving. As he irritatingly messed about with his smartphone, he breathed out clouds of smoke. At his feet on the pavement, where a NO SMOKING sign was painted, more than ten cigarette butts had accumulated. As Suka watched on, the man had already put another cigarette in his mouth and was pulling out his lighter.

"Oxy...gen...," muttered Suka in a deep voice as he put strength into his grip.

As if the imaginary clear ball Suka was "holding" had suddenly taken form, he felt a strong resistance pushing his fingers back. At the same time, the throbbing pulse coming from the thing inside his hand began to accelerate. With his joints starting to creak, Suka put all his strength and energy into his grip, and the imaginary ball slowly began to shrink.

"O-oxy...!!"

As sweat formed on Suka's forehead and the veins in his hand rose to the surface, the imaginary ball shrank to about five centimeters in diameter, but an overwhelming hardness kept his fingers from contracting any further.

Maybe this grip is more than I can handle, thought Suka, but if he couldn't manage at least this much, he would never get the results he wanted.

Through clenched teeth, Suka's abnormal voice rushed out. "...gen!! Oxy-gen!!!"

Leaning backward and pulling together all his strength, Suka was finally able to break through the invisible shell that was holding him back and grip his fingers together.

Through the gaps in Suka's fist, crimson beams of light shot forth. On the walkway down below, a sudden gust rushed by as people stumbled, pulling at their jackets and holding down their skirts, but that wind was merely a side effect.

The young businessman Suka had focused on, not seeming to notice the gust, placed his thumb on the flint wheel of his lighter as he brought it to his face. The spark from the struck flint flew toward the oil-soaked wick. The resulting flame burned ferociously, leaping more than thirty centimeters into the air. The flame not only burned away the man's cigarette but also engulfed his head and hair.

"Gyaaahhh!!!" The man's high-pitched screams could be heard even from where Suka stood, on the roof of that fifteen-floor building, and the screams from onlookers soon followed.

The businessman with his head on fire collapsed onto the pavement and squirmed, trying to put out the flame, but no matter what he did, it would not weaken or dissipate.

But of course. After all, that man was engulfed in a thick concentration of nearly 100 percent oxygen. With the power of the crimson sphere embedded in Suka's right fist, he had pulled all the oxygen from the surrounding air and concentrated it in that one spot.

Now, the pillar of fire had engulfed the businessman and had risen to a height of several meters. Leaves and garbage that had been pulled in by the gust of wind exploded as they instantly burned away, adding in a little extra flair.

"Kuh... Ku-ha-ha-ha-ha," chuckled Suka, unable to contain the laughter curdling deep within his throat.

Did you see that? Have you finally learned just how frightening and beautiful oxygen is?

In the midst of the flame, the businessman had stopped moving. His hands and feet melted and crumbled as he stood, and before long nothing remained but black carbonized ash. But still Suka would not release his grip. The flames heated the pavement until it glowed red, like lava. Who knows what the temperature had reached in the middle of that flame? But as long as there was material that could be oxidized, nothing would quell the intense anger of that oxygen.

Worship the flame, the beautiful phenomenon of oxidation.

Unable to run away, the idiotic onlookers had all fallen to their knees or collapsed. Of course, that was due to the fact the surrounding air was deprived of oxygen, but to Suka it looked as if they were bowing down in fear to the gigantic flame.

"Ha-ha-ha-ha-ha." Suka's thin body twisted as his shoulders shook with laughter.

Suka's power, which for a long time could only start a small flame, finally was able to burn away an entire human being. But this still wasn't enough.

It was not enough to cause the flames of Sodom that Suka needed in order to make humanity aware of its idiocy, aware of its wasteful synthesis of carbon dioxide from such a precious thing as oxygen.

Suka needed to take hold of the oxygen in an even wider area.

"Oxygen—! ♪ Oxygen—! ♪" he sang, finally releasing his grip.

"Oxy-oxy-oxygen—! ♪"

The skin in the center of Suka's right palm was split, opened up like an eye slit revealing a glossy wet sphere the color of blood. As the wind settled down below, a section of the brick pavement was now like glass, exposed to temperatures more than one thousand degrees Celsius. In the center of that, a single irregular black stain was all that remained.

2

Minoru Utsugi stepped out of the taxi and stared blankly at the rows of trees on either side of the road. Adjusting his scarf, which had started to slip, he turned to his fellow passenger, who had just left the taxi herself.

"...Is this the place?" he asked.

"This is it," said Yumiko Azu, nodding, with the hint of a mischievous smile as her glossy hair waved behind her.

Yumiko hadn't said a word since they'd left Yoshiki High School in Saitama City, Saitama, so Minoru thought she might have been upset, but that didn't seem to be the case.

Even so, Minoru didn't have the composure needed to give much thought to Yumiko's mood at the moment. After all, here he was, at the headquarters of the Ministry of Health, Labor, and Welfare's Industrial Safety and Health Department's Specialized Forces Division, the SFD. Yet this place Minoru was suddenly taken to go see, supposedly the headquarters of a secret organization founded to protect mankind, was a wooded area not unlike Akigase Park, located near Minoru's home in the Sakura district of Saitama.

"...Where in Tokyo are we anyway?" asked Minoru in a low voice to Yumiko, his SFD senior, after waiting for the taxi, along with the sound of its electric motor, to leave.

The taxi, which had picked Minoru up right outside of school, had spent nearly thirty minutes on the expressway connecting Saitama and the Tokyo metropolitan area, before making several turns after exiting, so Minoru, who had no experience with the area, had no idea where they were.

"This is actually part of Shinjuku," answered Yumiko before pointing a slender finger out toward the winter afternoon sky.

"West Waseda Station on the Fukutoshin line is over there, and over this way is Waseda Station on the Tozai line. I suppose we're about halfway between the two. By its address, headquarters is in Toyama 3-chome, Shinjuku," Yumiko continued.

"Shinjuku…"

The first things that came to Minoru's mind were the iconic twin towers of the Tokyo Metropolitan Government Building. Having seen those towers in photographs and on TV before, Minoru looked around to see if he could find them, but he couldn't see anything past the trees.

"Umm… So where is the Tokyo Metropolitan Government Building?" Minoru asked.

Minoru thought he had asked a serious question, but after staring dumbstruck at him for a moment, Yumiko looked as if she was trying to hold back laughter.

"There's no way we'd be able to see that from here. The Metropolitan Government Building is on the west side of Shinjuku Station, and where we are is basically the northeastern tip of the district," she finally answered.

"Oh… All right, then," muttered Minoru, nodding.

Was that really such a stupid question? In Saitama at least, you can see the tall buildings in the urban center from anywhere along the Arakawa River…, Minoru thought to himself.

"If there's time later, why don't you go walk around and familiarize yourself with the area?" Yumiko said, without offering to be a guide, and then lifted the backpack she was holding in her right hand and slung it over her shoulder.

"Come on, let's go," said Yumiko before starting off in a brisk walk down the sidewalk that ran along the trees.

It was Friday, December 13, exactly one week since Minoru had first encountered Yumiko at Akigase Park. Yumiko was wearing a black blazer, a gray pleated skirt, black tights, and mid-cut sneakers, just like she'd worn seven days before. Minoru couldn't tell, however, whether she had the same high-powered stun baton or combat knife hidden away under her skirt as she did then.

Having walked about ten meters ahead, Yumiko took a sudden left. When Minoru rushed to catch up to her, he saw an iron gate red with rust, which opened to a small path leading into the trees. After walking down that path for another ten seconds, crunching over leaves that had fallen over the asphalt, the path led to a wide square enclosure with trees on all sides. There, Minoru stopped dead in his tracks.

What stood quietly before him was a boxy, old five-story apartment building.

The outer wall of the building was concrete, and it looked like it had seen better days. About 30 percent of the building was covered in green moss, another 30 percent covered in vines, and the remaining 40 percent was dark from stains left over from the rain.

Minoru guessed that there were four apartments per floor, making a total of twenty units in the five-story building. Looking up at the verandas above, there were even clothes and mats hanging out to dry. There was nothing that looked secret or base-like about it.

Well, actually... I suppose that's the point, thought Minoru before timidly turning to Yumiko.

"So...does this mean there's a high-tech secret base hidden underground?" he asked.

"If you dug around here, all you'd find is a base for earthworms and pill bugs," answered Yumiko curtly. She walked ahead toward the building, and Minoru hurriedly followed after her.

When it comes to not looking the way you would expect, I suppose this building and Yumiko are the same. Who would expect this normal-looking girl in a school uniform to be hiding a stun baton, a large knife, and the ability to amplify acceleration? Not to mention the fact that she is the host of a "Jet Eye," a black Third Eye...

No, I need to stop.

Don't look. Don't think. Don't make any more memories.

Minoru pulled his gaze away from Yumiko and stared at the ground beneath his feet.

When one first starts learning about someone, those memories that form will demand to expand. Even more dangerous than wanting to know more about someone is how that emotion later translates into oneself wanting that person to know more about them.

The reason I came here, as the host of a Jet Eye, was not to fight the Ruby Eyes, nor was it to protect the people who inevitably become their victims. It was in order for me to reach a world, which I have been searching for for so long, where no one would know who I am. That is the only reason I am cooperating with them.

Minoru walked forward, tugging at the collar of his Chesterfield coat, which he had on over his school uniform.

Yumiko wordlessly walked ahead into the entrance of the apartment building and pressed the button on an old-looking elevator positioned at the back of the first floor. The elevator opened slowly and reluctantly, as if there was something wrong with the joints in the door.

The elevator was cramped and shook back and forth enough to make Minoru nervous several times as it went up. When Minoru looked at the area over the door, he could not find an inspection sticker. If that wasn't enough, for some reason the fragrance drifting over from Yumiko's hair as she stood diagonally in front of him made him feel even more nervous.

Now that I think about it...I had PE fifth period. I probably smell sweaty. I bet that's why she has her back turned to me, Minoru thought. He had just begun to consider activating his protective shell when the elevator finally reached the top floor.

The doors rumbled open and Minoru followed Yumiko out, pausing to take a short breath, and looked at his surroundings.

"Huh?!" Minoru gasped in surprise.

The first reason for his surprise was that the elevator did not lead out into a hall but opened immediately into a room. The second reason was that the room was incredibly spacious. There was a long distance between the left and right walls, and it appeared as if all of the interior walls on the fifth floor had been knocked out to make way for a large single room. The room spanned about 30 meters from east to west and 80 meters from north to south, which would mean the room had an area of 240 square meters. Given that one tatami mat is 1.6 square meters, this was a 150 tatami mat–size room.

The flooring was gray, and the walls and ceiling were bare concrete. Through the windows on the other side of the room, one could see the trees of the surrounding area glowing in the sunset. After pausing to look out those windows at a scene a person wouldn't expect to find in Shinjuku, right in the center of Tokyo, Minoru looked again around the room.

In a few words, Minoru thought the arrangement of the room was an incredible waste of the space. There was a large television and speaker set, a bookshelf that reached to the ceiling, a large sofa that could double as a bed, and a dining table that looked like it could seat ten people, all placed apart from one another, like lonely islands in the vastness of the room.

Minoru thought that his own room was relatively empty compared to what is normal for a high school boy, but the feeling of emptiness in this vast room was like that of the Kalahari Desert.

If he lived here, Minoru thought, he wouldn't have to go to the banks of the Arakawa River to run; he could just run around inside this room. As he continued to drift off into thought, Yumiko seemed to have lost her patience.

"I know that it's shocking and all, but are you done?" she snapped.

"Ah...y-yeah."

"Take off your shoes and change into these slippers."

Changing out of his sneakers as he was told, Minoru then followed Yumiko out into the large single room. Circling around the bookshelf, stepping over some cushions, and crossing in front of the TV, they walked fifteen meters to the western end of the room. This area alone looked fitting for a place called SFD Headquarters. There was a row of steel racks stuffed with computers, monitors, printers, scanners, drives, along with other mysterious instruments that Minoru didn't know what they were used for. There was also an experiment table with sinks attached, the kind you might find in a middle school science room, and on top of it were several things made of both glass and metal.

At the center of the table, looking into a large microscope, was...a child. There was no other way to put it. The young girl looked several years younger than Minoru. She couldn't have been even in middle school yet. She looked like she was maybe in her fourth or fifth year of elementary school. She had two small braids hanging down to her back and round freckled cheeks. She was wearing the kind of T-shirt one would expect an elementary school girl to wear, with a whitish denim mini-skirt. She had a name tag pinned to her chest with a safety pin and wore over her clothes a lab coat that looked like it reached to her ankles.

"Oh? Hmm...," the elementary school kid cutely mumbled.

"Professor! Pro-fes-sor!!" called out Yumiko in a loud voice.

Huh? Professor? You mean like the ones who teach at universities? thought Minoru confusedly, while Yumiko continued to raise her voice.

"Professor, I brought him! Your new guinea pi— I mean, our new SFD member!"

"Huh? Oh…I see," said the girl, finally raising her head from the microscope.

Still, this "professor" looked like any ordinary elementary school girl. She had pink cheeks and thick eyebrows and large eyes below them. Rather than wearing a lab coat and looking through a microscope, it would probably look more fitting for her to be running around outside in sportswear.

The girl hopped off the round stool she was sitting on, trotted in between the experiment table and steel racks, and then looked up at Minoru. To Minoru, that gaze felt as if it were piercing through to his very soul, and he twitched unconsciously.

As he stood there, Yumiko came and pushed Minoru from behind and entered the introduction phase.

"Utsugi, this is the deputy chief and strategic commander of the SFD, Riri Isa," Yumiko said.

Deputy chief? Strategic commander? Riri…Isa?

As Minoru stood there, confused, the girl's name tag came clearly into view. In cute lettering, it said, "Fourth Year, Class Two, Riri Isa."

The only schools in Japan that have a fourth year are elementary schools, technical colleges, and four-year universities, but the latter two just couldn't be possible.

"And this is Minoru Utsugi, who we were talking about before. You know, the one you were really interested in," Yumiko continued.

"You didn't have to add that, Yukko," Riri said with a smirk, taking her right hand out of her lab coat pocket and extending it to Minoru. Minoru reflexively grasped her hand; it was small and soft.

"I'm Isa, and I'm looking forward to working with you," said Riri.

"O-okay. Umm… I'm Minoru Utsugi. I'm looking forward to working with you, too," replied Minoru.

"All right! You can call me Deputy Isa, Riri, or Professor, like how Yukko does, or however else you want. In return, will you let me decide what to call you?" Riri asked.

While confused, Minoru didn't have any other options, so he nodded.

"Perfect!" Riri smiled this time with a more innocent-looking smile, and after pulling her hand back, she tilted her head in thought.

"Hmm… Utsugi… Ucchii… Tsugitsugi… Nope, we're going to have to use your first name… Minomino, Mirumiru… Norucchi…," Riri mumbled.

"Huh?"

Those couldn't possibly be nickname candidates, could they? Minoru shivered in thought, when Yumiko put her hand on his shoulder.

"Just accept it. I have to put up with the name Yukko after all. Professor really likes these sort of things, thinking about problems that have no answer," said Yumiko.

"Okay…?" replied Minoru.

Riri, who meanwhile had been walking back and forth in front of the table, suddenly clapped her hands together.

"I've got it! From now on, you will be called Mikkun!!"

Surely it was just a coincidence, but the name was very similar to "Mii-kun," the nickname Minoru's relative Norie Yoshimizu had given him, so Minoru thought it could have been a lot worse, but just then Yumiko burst into laughter.

"Well, you got a pretty cute nickname, didn't you?! I suppose I'll have to use it, too!" she laughed.

"Please don't," said Minoru in a flat-out rejection.

"I'm joking," said Yumiko in a serious tone before heading off into the kitchen area.

After this introduction phase was over and Yumiko had served coffee on the experiment table, the fourth-year elementary student deputy chief again openly looked Minoru over.

"Hmm... I've already seen photographs, but after meeting you directly...I really am surprised. To think that you were the one who took out Biter all on your own," said Riri in an awfully mature tone, but Minoru only shook his head.

"I-I didn't do it all by myself. When I fought Biter at the Saitama Super Arena, both Yumiko and DD were there," argued Minoru.

"You don't have to be modest. Not only were we late, we weren't able to help out at all. By the way, Professor, where did DD run off to?" asked Yumiko.

"He's apparently 'sniffed' another one out. He's searching along with Oli-V," answered Riri, stirring her cup of coffee full of milk and sugar.

Hearing Riri's answer, Yumiko's eyebrows twitched.

"Does that mean you're the only one here today? What about Lindenberger?" Yumiko asked.

"Absent as usual," Riri replied.

Who are Oli-V and Lindenberger?

And anyway, just how many Jet Eyes are there in the..."Ministry of Health, Labor, and Welfare Industrial Safety and Health Department, Specialized Forces Division"? Does this "professor" sitting right in front of me also have a Third Eye somewhere inside of her? If so, what is her ability?

Minoru began to feel dizzy. Maybe it was the flood of information he had received since coming to this apartment complex–turned-base or the number of questions that kept popping up inside his head. Since he usually lived by the motto "May today be no different than tomorrow," he realized he was weak against changes in environment. He wanted to learn the things he needed to know, then hurry back to his home in Saitama and reset his brain.

As if Riri had read Minoru's thoughts, she brought the conversation back to the subject at hand.

"Well, anyway, Mikkun. How much have you been told about the Third Eyes?" Riri asked.

"U-umm..." Minoru straightened his posture and looked down at the black surface of the experiment table. "They are spheres about two centimeters in diameter that come from space and infect human hosts... We don't know how many there are, but they come in two types: red 'Ruby Eyes' and black 'Jet Eyes.' The difference between them is that humans infected with Ruby Eyes are driven by a desire to kill other humans. Both types of Third Eyes give their human hosts mysterious powers. Like my shell or Yumiko's acceleration."

"Hmm. You've been told most of what there is to know. If I were to add one thing, it would be that one of the aspects of the powers Third Eyes give their hosts is no longer that mysterious," said Riri.

"What?" asked Minoru, holding the coffee cup that he was about to sip in midair. "You've discovered how the power works?!"

"Well...we haven't gotten that far yet. While we can vaguely hypothesize what is happening, we still have no way of describing how," answered Riri, shaking her head as she twisted one of her braids around her finger.

"B-but that's amazing! Just what is going on? What kind of power do Third Eyes possess?" asked Minoru, leaning forward.

Riri raised a finger in front of her. "Simply put, they're manipulating atoms and molecules. They're using some unexplained power similar to telekinesis."

"Manipulating...atoms?" pondered Minoru aloud.

"Exactly, and the effective range of that power is inversely related to the complexity of the atoms or molecules that are manipulated," continued Riri.

Riri then moved her right hand and passed Minoru a petri dish that was lying on the table. Inside was a shard of metal, about the size of a one-yen coin, which shined with a dull silver color Minoru was familiar with.

"Ah... Th-this is...," stuttered Minoru.

"One of Biter's teeth," continued Riri, crossing her arms. "It's incredible, really. There are molecules of iron and chromium organized in a nanoscale 3-D honeycomb structure within the normal hydroxylapatite crystal structure of the tooth, giving it an astonishing hardness of 2,500 on the Vickers scale."

"Excuse me, Professor. What is the hardness of a normal human tooth on the Vickers scale?" asked Yumiko.

Upon hearing that question, the fourth-year elementary school girl smiled as if to say, "Great question," before starting her explanation.

"Our teeth are at most a hardness of four hundred. Extremely hard metal alloys such as tungsten carbide are about 1,700 and sapphire 2,300. Does that help you understand just how hard Biter's teeth were? ...Coincidentally, there is no way to reproduce the material in that tooth with any existing technology we have today. The melting point of chromium is about 1,900 degrees Celsius, but the melting point of hydroxylapatite is 1,670 degrees. If you tried to coat a tooth in chromium, the tooth would burn away. In other words, to create these teeth, Biter manipulated iron, chromium, and hydroxylapatite concurrently. Not only that, but I hear that he altered the bones and muscle structures around his jaw as well."

"Ah... Th-that's correct," Minoru said, thinking back to the time he fought the Ruby Eye, Biter, just four days before. "It was as if his mouth stretched out like that of a shark..."

"Which means that he was able to alter the proteins, fats, calcium compounds, and other complex molecules that compose the human body at will. The Third Eyes who can alter human flesh like that generally can only use their powers on their own bodies," explained Riri.

"Ah... That's why you mentioned earlier that the effective range of power is inversely related to the complexity of what it affects," said Minoru, finding it strangely natural to speak to this elementary school girl in polite language.

Riri nodded with the air of a professor before continuing. "Exactly. You're catching on quick. To put it simply, the 'effective range' of Third Eye hosts who manipulate high molecular compounds made up of many atoms is short, but on the other hand, the simpler the molecules they manipulate, the longer the range of their power. If we split Third Eye powers into these two categories, Yukko's 'accelerator' power, for example, would fall into the same category as Biter's."

Yumiko, who had been listening, winced. "...Well, I mean, I am in a sense manipulating my entire body...but I don't do anything like transform...," she muttered.

"Well, I bet if you tried, you could," replied Riri with a smirk before continuing her explanation. "In Yukko's case, she uses the acceleration generated from kicking off ground as leverage to throw all of the molecules in her body forward.

"Therefore, according to the general rule, her power only affects her own body."

"She...throws her body?" repeated Minoru before turning to look at Yumiko. Yumiko in her black blazer sipped her coffee and pretended not to notice.

Minoru had seen Yumiko, code name "Accelerator," perform teleport-like dashes several times when they fought Biter, but he had thought her power was manipulating acceleration itself. Even when it was explained to him as her throwing all of the molecules that make up her body, he had trouble grasping the concept.

As he tried his best to comprehend, furrowing his brow, Riri cut in unexpectedly.

"It looks like Mikkun's having trouble, so why don't we show him an example of your power at work, Yukko?" Riri said.

"What? Here?" said Yumiko, obviously against the idea, but Riri nodded, unaffected.

"If he takes a look at what happens one more time, I'm sure he'll understand in an instant," she said.

"Utsugi's already seen me use my power several times, though," Yumiko said but stood up from her chair.

Prompted by Riri, Minoru stood up as well.

"Mikkun, you should probably stand and watch from a distance... Over there will be fine," said Riri.

"O-okay."

As he was instructed, Minoru moved over near where the TV was, in the center of the south side of the giant room, which was about fifteen meters away from the experiment table along the west wall. It wouldn't have felt like such a long distance outdoors, but indoors, Minoru felt as if he were very far away.

"All right, let's go! Watch closely now, Mikkun!" Riri called out.

"I'm the one who's doing the jumping, though," said Yumiko, who took off her slippers, looking as if she had given up. Her two feet wrapped in black tights stepped lightly on the flooring as if she were testing its hardness.

Yumiko lifted her arms out and behind her, perhaps to cut wind resistance, and put her right foot forward.

But her foot didn't touch the ground. As if it were being pulled by an invisible rubber sling, Yumiko's body went hurtling forward at an incredible speed, hovering a few centimeters off the ground, flying past Minoru with a whoosh of wind.

Minoru wasn't able to follow Yumiko with his eyes as she landed on the other side of the room. It wasn't that his eyes couldn't keep up, but that after seeing Yumiko's white blouse pressed strongly against her chest from the air pressure of the leap, the image burned into his brain and cut his train of thought.

But wait, what happened to the blazer that she was just wearing? Minoru thought.

Two seconds later, the answer was clear.

"J-just what do you think you're doing, Professor?!" squealed Yumiko, using her power to fly back to the west side of the room, where Riri was standing with a black blazer in her right hand and a mischievous smile on her face.

Riri had probably grabbed the back of Yumiko's blazer right before Yumiko dashed forward. Because Yumiko had lifted both her arms behind her, it must have easily come off and was left in Riri's hand.

"Give it back!" Yumiko took back her blazer as soon as she landed, but in her rush to put it back on, her hand got caught in the left sleeve and she was having trouble. Minoru looked away as he headed back to the experiment table.

With both of her hands stuffed in her lab coat pockets, Riri smiled at Minoru. "So, do you understand now?" she asked.

"Umm..."

"Just what was it that you wanted me to understand by showing me that?" wondered Minoru before reaching the answer.

If Yumiko's power was as Minoru had originally thought and was the power to directly amplify acceleration, it should affect everything undergoing the original acceleration. However, just by Riri, who was by no means large, grabbing hold of Yumiko's blazer, it easily came off and was left behind. In other words...

"This means that...Yumiko's power only works on her own body, and her clothing is just being pulled along?" asked Minoru.

"Exactly!" exclaimed Riri with a snap of her fingers as she helped Yumiko put her blazer back on.

"The polar opposite of those like Yukko and the Biter who

use their powers to manipulate themselves are those like DD who use their power for remote sensing."

Minoru thought back to the face of that young man with his sleepy-looking eyes. His power was the ability to sniff out other Third Eyes, and he was chasing after Biter along with Yumiko. The one who gave him the cool nickname "DD" was probably Riri. *If so, I wonder what Oli-V and Lindenberger's real names are...*

As Minoru began to drift off, Riri's voice brought him back into focus.

"DD can't manipulate any molecules at all, but in return, he can sense molecules that are manipulated by other Third Eyes several kilometers away. You could say that it's a power that specializes in range, having given up both potential for attack and defense," Riri explained.

"Ha-ha... It sounds like we're discussing where to put our status points in an RPG...," Minoru said.

"You seem like you would get along pretty well with the other guy, don't you?" said Yumiko, having finished putting on her blazer and buttoning it securely from top to bottom.

"Huh? Y-you mean DD?" asked Minoru.

"No, the other guy," answered Yumiko.

Huh? Who is she talking about? thought Minoru, but without clarifying, Yumiko turned to Riri.

"But enough of all that, Professor. Can we get to the main reason we came all this way? The sun's going to set," she said.

"The time the sun will set in Tokyo on December 13, 2019, is at sixteen hundred hours twenty-eight minutes and forty-three seconds. We only have five minutes left, but I guess we can hurry along," said the maybe ten-year-old Riri, without looking at a calendar or smartphone. She motioned for Minoru and Yumiko to sit back down on their round stools before taking a seat herself across from them and taking a sip of her coffee filled with milk.

"Now that we've finished all of the formalities, Mikkun, about your power...," started Riri.

"R-right...," answered Minoru, straightening up.

"When Yukko first described your power as a protective shell, I hypothesized that you were using molecules to create a clear barrier. As part of the investigation to learn what molecules those were, I analyzed Biter's tooth. Biter bit down several times on your protective barrier, so I thought that there should be some residue of your shell left on the surface of the tooth," Riri continued.

"Ah...okay...," said Minoru, nodding, remembering his frightening experiences from four days before. Biter had transformed his head into that of a man-eating shark's with silver teeth that could bite through iron, and he had used those teeth several times in an attempt to destroy Minoru's shell. If Minoru's shell were made up of some clear material, then some of the molecules should have been scraped away by the teeth.

But Riri looked over at the petri dish on the table with an unsatisfied look on her face.

"However, it appears I was wrong. The only material I recovered from this tooth was concrete fragments from the underground parking lot of the Saitama Super Arena, where you had your last battle with Biter. Nothing else could be detected with an electron microscope or a gas chromatography test. I cannot imagine a shell could endure being bitten by teeth harder than any other substance but diamond and sustain absolutely no damage," explained Riri.

"...Ah," muttered Yumiko after a pause. Though she had looked upset ever since she had her blazer stripped from her, all traces of that were gone, and she brought her hands together with her fingers intertwined.

"Then couldn't it just be made out of diamond? Diamond is crystallized carbon, right? If his power manipulates carbon, he could just take it from the carbon dioxide in the surrounding air... Is there any possibility he is crystallizing that carbon at will to form a shell?" offered Yumiko.

"Hmm. That is a very interesting point, and that would be fascinating, but..." Riri shrugged her shoulders and smiled in an unchildlike, cynical smile. "Unfortunately, while diamond excels at hardness, its toughness, or shatter resistance, isn't especially high. Even if you were to make a thin shell out of diamond, a normal person could break it to pieces with one swing of an ordinary hammer. I doubt that it could withstand the stress put on it by the Biter's bite."

"Well, that's no fun," said Yumiko disappointedly as she sipped her cold coffee.

Riri lifted two fingers toward Minoru, who was starting to feel like a letdown.

"Therefore, I made a second hypothesis that your defensive shell is not made of any material but is a form of molecular manipulation all by itself," Riri continued.

"Molecular...manipulation?" repeated Minoru.

"How should I explain it...? Ah, look at this," Riri said, bringing the petri dish with Biter's tooth back in front of her. After removing the lid, she took a pair of tweezers and pressed on the top of the tooth.

When she did this the tooth, about two centimeters in diameter, split in two from left to right. The surface of the cut shined like a mirror.

"That's amazing! How did you do that?!" exclaimed Minoru, reaching out his right hand toward the petri dish.

"Don't touch it! The edge of the cut is so sharp you'll cut yourself just by touching it!" Riri immediately warned, and Minoru drew back his hand.

"O-okay... Prof— I mean, Ms. Isa, did you just cut that tooth?" asked Minoru.

"You can call me Professor if you want, and the answer to that question is no. It had already been cut but was being held together by van der Waals forces."

"Van der Waals forces...," repeated Minoru.

In Minoru's science class, they had covered the basics about those forces as part of their physics curriculum.

"You mean intermolecular forces, right? But I thought in order for something like metal to be held together by only those forces, the surfaces between the two halves would have to be perfectly smooth and even... Did you cut Biter's tooth with a diamond cutter and polish the halves for some reason? Why?" asked Minoru.

"Good question," Riri said, nodding. "Certainly, cutting this tooth by normal means would require a diamond cutter, but in this case, this tooth was cut by abnormal means. Specifically, it was cut using the power of one of the members of the SFD."

"...!" Minoru gasped and stared at the petri dish with the two halves of the tooth. Cutting Biter's tooth like that into halves like it was cheese certainly was abnormal.

"By power do you mean...the power to create a blade like a razor that is as hard as diamond...?"

"Now that was not a good question," said Riri with a smirk on her face, twirling her pointer finger around as if she were reeling in the conversation. "Didn't I just say that your shell is not made out of a material, but instead might be a form of the manipulative power itself? The power that cut this tooth is the same kind of power. For the sake of simplicity, we call the power 'division,' but...simply put, the power nullifies the intermolecular forces within an object along a certain plane. The couplings between molecules are cut, so whether the object was a clump of hardened steel or a block of tofu, it will be perfectly cut in two."

"Division...huh," muttered Minoru, lost in thought.

Riri looked down at the petri dish on the table before speaking again. "So have you figured out what I'm trying to say? That like this division power, your protective shield is not made out of any material, but is..."

"Ah...I see. It's not a material, but the power itself... In other words, it's a power that rejects molecules?" asked Minoru.

"Precisely!" exclaimed Riri, clapping her hands together. "That was my second hypothesis. It puts your power as being the same type as division, while being put to a completely different use. If that were the case, it would explain why Biter's teeth were unable to scrape off a single molecule from your protective shell. However...and this is the catch..." Riri paused before doubling back on her argument just as it was making sense to Minoru.

"When I read the report about your final battle with Biter, I had to reject my second hypothesis...," Riri said.

"What...? Wait, but why?" asked Minoru.

"That is because you were able to isolate yourself from even the fierce heat of that gasoline fire!" exclaimed Riri, biting down on her lip with her pearl-like teeth.

Riri suddenly stood up and grabbed an LED desk lamp from the table and flipped the switch, pointing orange light that came out of it at Minoru's right hand. Minoru could feel warmth emanating from the spot that was lit.

"The heat you feel radiating from a flame is not a material substance but a series of electromagnetic waves, the same as the heat radiating from this lamp. So let us assume that your defensive shell isolates you from electromagnetic waves. However, visible light is also made up of electromagnetic waves. For that argument to make any sense, you would have to be unable to see outside your shell when it was activated, and others would have to be unable to see inside your shell as well. If your shell absorbed light, it would be pitch-black, and if it reflected light, it would be like a mirror, right?!" argued Riri.

As Minoru was trying to keep up with the increasing difficulty of the conversation, his mind was drawn back to his frightening battle with that shark man, Biter.

When Biter's brains were blown out, his Third Eye had gone berserk, transforming him into even more of a monster. With his fanged arms, he had ripped the frame of an automobile into pieces, as if it were made of paper. As gasoline poured over Biter's head from the ruptured fuel tank, Minoru had rushed in, using his defensive shell to pin down Biter, and he had gotten Yumiko to provide a spark from her stun baton.

The gasoline immediately caught fire, and crimson flames had engulfed both Biter and Minoru. At the time, Minoru certainly felt more than enough fear, but he hadn't felt any change in heat.

In other words, Minoru's defensive shell had completely rejected the heat from that flame burning at close range. But even so, Minoru had seen the bright light of the flames, and to have one without the other didn't make any sense. After all, the red light from the flame was made up of the same electromagnetic waves that carry thermal energy.

Turning off the desk lamp, Riri's eyes sparkled as she continued at a fast pace.

"Of course, that doesn't mean I'm out of ideas for hypotheses! For example, it could be that your defensive shell only lets through electromagnetic waves that fall within a certain safe range of wavelengths that include visible light. If that were the case, it would mean that your power does not only work on the order of molecules, but it also affects subatomic particles, but I can't say anything for sure until we run some tests," Riri said excitedly.

Then, Minoru timidly raised his right hand, a single doubt having surfaced in the back of his mind.

"Umm… Ms.…Professor?" he asked.

"What is it, Mikkun? If you're going to call me Professor, you don't have to add a Ms.," Riri replied.

"Ah, sorry about that…Professor. When I am using my power, I can see outside just fine, but I can't hear a sound. Does that mean that I am rejecting all of the air molecules that would vibrate to carry sound? Like oxygen and nitrogen?" asked Minoru.

"Hmm. That seems like a plausible explanation," replied Riri.

"However…a few days ago I had my power activated for more than an hour, but…when I think about it now, I didn't have trouble breathing at all. Doesn't that sound contradictory…?" continued Minoru.

"…" Riri froze, her eyebrows coming close together. "What did you just say?"

Over the next two hours, Professor Riri Isa thoroughly investigated the properties of Minoru's defensive shell herself.

It grew dark outside the windows, and beyond the tree line was visible the shine of lights set up for the holiday season in east Shinjuku. Yumiko had lain down on the sofa a little ways away and was immersed in reading a comic series.

Minoru had told Norie, his adoptive elder sister, that he was staying over at a friend's house. From Norie's perspective, Minoru hadn't done anything like that in the eight years he had stayed with her, and she was thrilled. But of course, Minoru wasn't exactly telling the truth and felt bad about it. Yumiko offered to talk on the phone to corroborate his story, but it went without saying that Minoru politely refused.

As he continued to muse vaguely about these things, Minoru activated his power several times on a table surrounded by video cameras and odd sensors.

Riri groaned several times in thought as she continued to

take measurements, but by the time the clock struck seven o'clock at night, she declared that she was done for the day.

After Minoru leaped down from the table and was putting on his shirt, Yumiko headed over toward him with a large yawn.

"Are you finally done? Professor, let's go ahead and have dinner. I'm starving," said Yumiko, now without her blazer, which she had taken off earlier, along with the ribbon for her blouse.

"I don't mind, but DD hasn't come back yet, and that means that one of us is going to have to be the ones to prepare it," said Riri.

"Geh... You're right...," said Yumiko, her face twitching a bit as she looked up at the ceiling. "I really don't want to have a repeat of that tragedy we had before..."

...*Tragedy?* thought Minoru, puzzled.

Yumiko then glared angrily out the window and yelled, "Argh! If only we could order delivery!!"

"Huh...? You mean we can't order delivery?" asked Minoru reflexively. They were in Shinjuku and it was only seven o'clock. They should have no problem ordering pizza or sushi or Chinese food... There should have been tons of options.

But glancing back at Minoru, Yumiko just shook her head. "We can't. After all, no one is able to enter this area."

"What do you mean? After all, the gate leading to this place was wide open when we got here," said Minoru.

"Chief Himi has set up a barrier that extends all the way to the gate. Even if an outsider crosses the road in front of the gate, they can't perceive that there is a gate or an apartment complex here. We could pick something up if we had it delivered somewhere around Meiji Street, but if we're going to go that far, we might as well go eat out," continued Yumiko.

"A barrier..." Minoru finally understood what she was referring to. Chief Himi was a man with a sort of warrior-like air that Minoru had been introduced to at a hospital in Saitama four days ago. He was the commander in chief of the SFD, and his power was the ability to manipulate people's memories.

Since Third Eye powers work on atoms and molecules, Himi's power probably had something to do with synapses and neurons in the brain, but who would have thought that he could make this five-story building imperceptible to outsiders, without even being here...

"...I'm starting to think that there are no limits to what these powers can do...," muttered Minoru before lifting his head and noticing that Yumiko was staring at him from a very close distance.

"Uwah!" Minoru shouted, pulling back. "Wh-what's the matter?!"

"Hey, Uuutsuuugiiii...," said Yumiko.

"...What is it?" he repeated.

"You don't happen to be able to cook, do you?" asked Yumiko.

"A-as long as it's something simple...," stuttered Minoru in response.

But by the time he had realized his mistake, Yumiko had already grabbed Minoru firmly by the shirt collar.

"It's not like I'm asking you to make a full-course French meal, or a Kyoto-style ceremonial dinner, or a Manchu-Han imperial Chinese feast, as long as you just make something edible!" exclaimed Yumiko before going behind Minoru and pushing him toward the kitchen on the other side of the room.

"Mikkun, I don't like chrysanthemums or shiitake mushrooms," said Riri, waving her hand without looking away from the monitor she was working at.

...If only she weren't a fourth-year elementary school girl, I would have made a hot pot filled to the brim with chrysanthemums and shiitake mushrooms, thought Minoru to himself as he crossed the thirty-meter room.

The peninsula-style kitchen was surprisingly well fitted out. There were three built-in-type gas stoves, and the stainless steel countertop was well polished. The faucet had a water purification device attached to it, and the hanging shelves had several thick pots and frying pans.

"...Is it okay for me to use this...?" asked Minoru.

Yumiko nodded. "DD bought all of these things on his own whim and with the SFD's budget to boot, so I won't let him complain."

"Okay..."

When Minoru went to open the German Miele-made large-form refrigerator, it was stocked full of fresh ingredients. With this much at his disposal, Minoru would be able to make do with his small repertoire of recipes. After turning to Yumiko one more time to say that he didn't guarantee it would taste any good, he took a large stockpot, filled it with water, and put it on the stove.

Then he defrosted some squid, clams, and shelled shrimp in the microwave and prepared a smaller pot of boiling water to parboil some asparagus and broccoli. By the time he had finished that, the water in the large pot had begun to boil, so he added a large amount of salt and dried pasta for three people.

After that, he minced a clove of garlic and put it in a frying pan with olive oil, along with chili peppers he had removed the seeds from, and set it to low heat. When the garlic started to faintly colorize, he added the seafood and vegetables and quickly fried them. When the heat had started to pass evenly through the ingredients, he added water from the boiling pot of pasta and shook the ingredients around. The thick frying pan was probably about two kilograms, but perhaps with the help of his Third Eye strengthening his muscles, it didn't feel heavy at all.

When the oil in the pan started to get cloudy, he turned to Yumiko, who was standing beside him.

"I'm sorry, but could you take those tongs over there and strain the pasta?"

"Oh—sure," she replied.

Minoru took the pasta that Yumiko had clumsily moved with tongs from the pot to a strainer and dumped it into the frying pan with the stove on full heat. The pasta hissed with steam as Minoru agitated the pan, mixing the emulsified sauce and pasta and adding a little salt to fine-tune the flavor.

"Could you bring over the plates please?" said Minoru.

"O-okay!" Yumiko replied.

After adding pepper from a pepper grinder, he took the frying pan and evenly distributed its contents among the three plates Yumiko set next to the stove. Then, after sprinkling a bit of a sweet basil leaf he ripped in his hands, he took a final sigh.

"...Well, anyway. It's done," Minoru said to the sound of applause.

Riri, who at some point had come to the entrance of the kitchen, and Yumiko standing beside her were clapping.

"...He did it in just fifteen minutes, Professor," said Yumiko.

"I'm surprised as well... When DD's chef, it always takes at least an hour...," replied Riri.

"Um, I mean," said Minoru, shaking his head. "It's only that way because I was skipping some steps."

Minoru lived alone with Norie, who was busy working at the Saitama Prefectural Office, so not only did he often help prepare meals, but also there were many times he made them himself.

It wasn't as if Minoru disliked cooking, but as a high school boy, he was more concerned with recipes for "food that you can make fast that has plenty of volume and is reasonably edible," and this heavy-volume *peperoncino* was no exception. Taste was a secondary factor. However...

After taking their own dishes to the dining table that sat next to the kitchen, Yumiko and Riri wolfed down the food as if they were competing with each other. He was happy to have other people eat his food, but at the same time he hated himself for feeling that way. If he felt happy about being praised despite the fact that he didn't want to have any memories shared with other people, it would be incredibly hypocritical.

When I get back home, I'll forget this...and to help me forget, I won't make peperoncino *for a while,* Minoru thought to himself as he ate.

While Minoru was thinking these negative thoughts, Yumiko finished eating and gulped down the rest of her oolong tea and sighed a deep sigh of satisfaction.

"I don't think I've had food that tasted like this in a long while...," she said.

"Agreed. It must be a flavor that you can only bring out with speed...," Riri added.

Minoru shook his head again. "I-I'm sorry, I have no idea how to make a proper meal..."

"No, we're complimenting you, Utsugi. This pasta is very delicious. It has a very nostalgic flavor...," said Yumiko with a rare clear smile, but that just made Minoru feel more embarrassed.

Where do these two live, anyway? Minoru wondered. *It might be all right for Yumiko, who is a high school student, to be out and about, but isn't it about time for an elementary school student like Professor to go home?*

Minoru hurried to swallow the squid in his mouth to ask about it, but before he could, Yumiko changed the subject.

"So...Professor. What did you find out about Minoru's defensive barrier?" she asked.

Riri, who had been twirling a piece of broccoli on the end of her fork in the air, groaned.

"Well...I did find out one thing, and that is with the equipment I have here now, I can't figure anything out," she said.

"What? I can't believe there's something that you can't understand!" Yumiko exclaimed.

"Of course there are some things I can't understand, Yukko," replied Riri with a cynical smile before popping the piece of broccoli into her mouth. "My power is not the power to find the answer to any given question, after all."

Having heard that, Minoru stared at the small girl sitting across from him at the table.

"...So does that mean you are a Third Eye host as well, Professor? Just what kind of power do you have?" asked Minoru.

The answer to that question was simple but unexpected.

"It's thinking," replied Riri.

"Thinking...?" repeated Minoru, confused.

"Professor's power is the power of 'speculation.' For almost any question that has an answer, she can find that answer almost immediately. Even if that is, for example, the prime factorization of a number with hundreds of decimal places," clarified Yumiko.

"This power is nothing special; any computer given enough time can accomplish the same thing... To be honest, I think that as a result of this power I've become an utter fool... but that's enough about me," said Riri.

Taking a sip of grapefruit juice, Riri brought the conversation back on topic.

"After taking various measurements, I have come to the conclusion that Mikkun's defensive shell is not made out of any actual material. For one, the coefficient of friction on its surface is absolutely zero," said Riri.

"Zero...friction...?" repeated Minoru, unable to imagine immediately what that would mean.

Yumiko made an objection in his place.

"But Professor, that doesn't make any sense! Utsugi has run with his shell activated. If there were no friction, he wouldn't be able to kick off from the ground and would slip and fall on the spot," she argued.

"That is true, but it doesn't seem that Mikkun is actually standing on the ground when he has his shell activated," Riri replied.

"What? ...But then how is he able to stand?" Yumiko rebutted.

"I have no idea. I can't say anything else until I finish analyzing the data," Riri replied before putting the last bite of her pasta in her mouth and savoring it. "Thank you, that was delicious," she finally said, smiling at Minoru.

"N-no, it was nothing...," said Minoru.

"No, no, it was fantastic. It's enough to make me want to give you the code name 'Cooker,'" Riri replied.

Yumiko burst out laughing. "DD would hate you if you did that. He's totally serious about his cooking."

"Code name... You mean like how Yumiko's is 'Accelerator'?" asked Minoru.

"Exactly. You already know that our organization gives code names to Ruby Eyes that we identified, right?" said Riri.

"Yes, like 'Biter,'" said Minoru.

"Correct. All of our organization's members also have code names. After all, it's dangerous to use your real names in the middle of combat. Yukko's code name is 'Accelerator.' The one who split Biter's tooth's code name is 'Divider.' DD's is 'Searcher,' and mine is 'Speculator.' Now that you've become a member, we'll need to think of a code name for you as well... 'Defender' doesn't really fit well... 'Hardener' makes you sound like a cosmetic nail product... Hmm...," Riri said as she mused.

"...What about 'Isolator'?" offered Yumiko in a quiet voice.

After blinking a few times, Riri looked troubled. "Don't you think that's a bit too tongue-in-cheek?" she said.

"Not at all. When all of the Ruby Eyes are exterminated and the SFD is disbanded, Utsugi is going to have the memories of himself from every other human being removed by Chief Himi... That was his condition for joining us," Yumiko argued. With a faint smile, she continued. "So we will one day forget the pasta that we ate today. It won't remain in anyone's memory... Don't you think that is sad?"

Riri apparently hadn't been told of Minoru's condition for joining. Her eyes opened wide and stared at Minoru for a while, but finally with a tolerant smile well beyond her years, she nodded. "...I see. Mikkun, do you have any objections to being called 'Isolator'?"

"No." Minoru quickly shook his head. "I think it's a good name. Isolator, huh...? I like it."

"Well, then, I'll make a record of your new code name. But still, if I knew that I was going to forget the flavor of this pasta, I wish I could have savored it more," Riri said.

Minoru didn't have any response to give her, but after a short pause Yumiko said, "I'm sure he'll make it again for us."

3

After Ayato Suka locked the door of his apartment behind him, he took a deep breath.

It was sweet.

The thick oxygen in the air made its way through his lungs to his blood vessels and spread all throughout his body, cleaning away the pollution of the outside world.

Suka had filled every room of his two-bedroom apartment with potted plants, both large and small. But none of them were the kind of plants that withered after flowering for a short time, the kind of plants cultivated just to serve human ego. They were all reliable plants thick with glossy leaves of deep green, vigorously photosynthesizing.

Taking several deep breaths before he was content, Suka finally removed his leather shoes. As he entered the living room, overflowing with green, he immediately opened the glass door opening to the south veranda, where there were so many green potted plants there was no place to step. In order to make the best of the shorter daylight hours in the winter, Suka moved plants from inside his apartment to the veranda every morning on a rotation schedule.

However, no matter how much the Tokyo metropolis was becoming a subtropical climate, if he didn't move the plants inside as soon as the sun set, they were in danger of being damaged by the frost. It was a lot of work to move the dozens of potted plants to and from the veranda every morning and evening, but that didn't bother Suka. After all, it was for the sake of the plants he had worked so hard on, and because of the red eye he hosted inside of his body, both his strength and stamina had risen considerably.

"It was cold out there, wasn't it? Don't worry, I'll warm you right up," Suka whispered to a Strelitzia plant with thick extended leaves, as he rolled up his sleeves and set about his work.

By the time Suka had moved the fifth plant from the veranda to its spot inside by the wall, he was interrupted as a loud electric sound rang over the intercom.

"..." He paused, frowning. He looked at the LCD monitor on the wall, but there was no video. He wasn't being called from the front of the building, but from the bell in front of his door.

It's probably a solicitor who slipped in through the auto-locked front area as another resident was passing through, he thought and decided to ignore the bell. But just as he was about to return to his work, there was a loud knock on the door accompanied by a loud and irritated voice.

"Mr. Suka, it's Ooshima from next door! I know you're home!" the voice called.

Suka clicked his tongue. It was the housewife who lived one room to his right, and he knew why she was here. He tried ignoring her, but she wouldn't stop knocking on the door. With a sigh, Suka finally stopped his work and walked toward the door.

"Hey, I know you're there! I just heard you out on the veranda!" the woman yelled.

To at least convey some of his irritation, he roughly and loudly flipped the lock to the door. Opening the door as little as possible, so that she wouldn't see into his apartment, Suka stepped out into the hallway and turned to face Mrs. Ooshima.

The round middle-age woman wearing glasses with colored lenses shook her drooping cheeks with anger as she yelled, "Mr. Suka, I've already told you several times before not to put your plants out on the veranda, haven't I? But today, when I looked around the barrier between our apartments...it looks like a jungle out there! Lately these disgusting bugs have been coming over to our veranda, and I bet they're coming from your side! Just where is your common sense?!"

...*You peeked around the barrier?* Suka thought, trying to control the anger lurking in his throat before making the same argument he made three days ago.

"As I am aware, according to the rules laid down by the management, tenants are allowed to put decorative plants out on their verandas."

"That doesn't mean that you can go and make your veranda a forest!!" Mrs. Ooshima screeched. "When people see that forest from the outside, it's an embarassment to the entire apartment complex! How are you going to take responsibility if the property value falls?! Plus, even if it's allowed to put plants on the veranda, there's nothing saying it's okay to raise bugs!!"

Suka's irritation spread from his chest to his right shoulder and down to his right hand. In his clenched fist, that object started to give off a gentle heat.

I'll burn you to ash, you old hag, thought Suka, fireworks going off deep inside his mind. But with a deep breath, he was somehow able to calm himself down.

"But Mrs. Ooshima. From what I can tell looking at your veranda from outside, you seem to have several potted plants as well," Suka said in a low voice, objecting once more. In reality, on the Ooshimas' veranda there were several large potted plants, even if it wasn't to the extent Suka maintained.

However, many of the plants she was keeping outside, such as anthurium and areca palms, had a low tolerance to cold and most of their leaves had fallen away. It was a pitiful reflection of her, but more than that, he felt sorry for the plants.

"...By the way, I wanted to tell you that the anthuriums you have can't survive outside in the winter like this, so until it gets warmer, I think you should move them inside...," Suka started.

"You've been peeking into my veranda?! H-how obscene!!" Mrs. Ooshima suddenly shrieked, her thick lips and cheeks shivering. "We have a young daughter living at home with us! I can't believe you were peeking! The police! I need to call the police!"

Wait a minute, Suka thought. *Aren't you the one who just said something about the way my veranda looks lowering property values? Even before that, didn't you say that you were peeking around the barrier to look at my veranda?*

His shock only lasted a moment before his anger came back twofold, like a spasm running through his back.

I want to burn her, he thought. *I want to burn this lowly, ignorant, sad excuse for a living thing until there's nothing of her left but a small black stain.*

But even without going that far, all I would have to do is grasp the air around her and deprive her of oxygen until she fainted. After all, right now her ugly dilated nose and mouth are sucking in air like a vacuum cleaner, he thought.

But no, now wasn't the time. He couldn't yet use his power within the scope of his home, workplace, or his route to work. Suka was warned that there were those who hunted red Third Eye hosts, hosts with black Third Eyes... That was also when he learned that this thing was called a Third Eye.

The black hunters could detect when reds used their powers from a great distance away and would come to attack them.

In the beginning, back when he didn't know anything about the Third Eyes, when Suka believed that he was the only one endowed with this power, he was attacked once by the black hunters. He was barely able to get away by depriving one of their members of oxygen, but before that he had been heavily wounded.

Of course, he intended to take revenge, especially on the one girl who drove a knife deep into his stomach. If nothing else, he would make sure she burned. It was for that sake that he trained in the mountains to strengthen his power. He would look for an opportunity, plan and set a meticulous trap, and beautifully oxidize her.

So now was not the time for him to be consumed by petty rage.

Breathing in air deep to the depths of his lungs, Suka visualized the oxygen purifying his blood and faced the hysterical woman with a level tone. "If you feel you must call the police, then do as you will. As for plants on my veranda, let us bring it up at the next management meeting. Good night."

Shutting the middle-age woman's screeching voice out of his mind, he returned to his apartment and shut the door. He turned the lock and returned to his living room. Even while he continued about his work moving his plants, the spark of anger in his chest would not completely go out.

But that is fine for now, Suka thought.

Anger magnifies strength. In order for me to take my revenge on the black hunters, I need to grasp an even wider area of oxygen. It's not enough that I can only just barely burn a single person away, he thought. *I need to be able to call forth the great fires of Sodom that burned those very skies and burn them all in a single sweep like insects that fly into a flame.*

Having finished carrying all the potted plants in from the veranda, he shut the glass door and stood in the middle of his green-filled living room with his arms spread wide. He took in with his entire body the great volumes of oxygen ejected from the plants that had bathed in sunlight all day.

"Ohh...," he sighed in ecstasy, curling the fingers of his right hand. The crimson eye in the middle of his palm pulsed happily.

4

After they had finished eating, Riri quickly returned to the experiment area and Yumiko said that she would clean up and took the dishes into the kitchen.

Minoru, left at the dining table, stared blankly out the window at the nightly scene of east Shinjuku. Once he heard a loud clanging sound from the kitchen, but he carefully decided to pretend he didn't hear anything.

A few minutes later, Yumiko returned with two steaming mugs.

"Here you go," she said.

"Ah, thank you," Minoru replied, taking his cup with a nod. At first glance, it appeared to be coffee, but as he brought the cup closer to check how it smelled, Yumiko glared at him from across the table.

"You don't have to be that rude. Even I can prepare coffee, you know? Instant coffee at least," she said, taking out a couple of packs of sweeteners from her skirt pocket and setting them on the table. "Here, use whichever you like."

"All right...," said Minoru, taking a pack of gum syrup, wondering if it was really all right to put one of these in hot coffee, but as Yumiko seemed to do so with no problem, Minoru followed suit. *I suppose gum syrup's sweetening effect doesn't change, no matter what you put it in*, he thought.

After they both took a sip, Yumiko spoke. "I'm sorry about earlier."

"...What do you mean?" he asked.

"For deciding your code name for you. It's still not too late if you want to change it now...," said Yumiko, acting unusually meek, but Minoru shook his head.

"No, it's fine. I wasn't lying when I said I liked it. I think the name Isolator is really fitting," he said.

It seemed that Yumiko based the name Isolator on Minoru's wish to be in "a world where no one knew him," but whenever Minoru activated his defensive shell, he truly was put in complete isolation. Cut off from the rest of the world, the only thing that could reach him from the outside was light. He couldn't think of any other word more fitting to describe that state than *isolation*.

"I mean, it actually sounds kind of cool. I'm not sure I can live up to the name," he added.

Minoru didn't think he had said anything out of the ordinary, but for some reason, Yumiko looked upset.

"...Well, if you don't have a problem with it, I don't mind," she said before taking a large sip of coffee and almost spitting it out with a gasp because it was too hot.

Just what does she want from me? Minoru thought to himself.

Women had all been an utter mystery to Minoru from as long as he could remember, but especially with Yumiko, he had no idea where her mood would turn. It was like riding on a roller coaster in pitch darkness. This was fitting, perhaps, for someone named Accelerator. But as he was pondering this, his thoughts were interrupted by Yumiko.

"Umm... Utsugi? I was just wondering, but...," she said.

"Wh-what?" Minoru replied.

"Let's assume there was a girl out there who was madly in love with you," she continued.

"Wait, what?!" Minoru reflexively jerked back, but Yumiko waved her hand in front of her face with a serious look to calm him down.

"I'm not talking about me. This is a 'what if' scenario. Anyway. Assuming there was a girl like that, would you want to erase all of her memories of you as well?" Yumiko asked.

"I would," Minoru quickly replied, and this time it was Yumiko who jerked back about five centimeters.

"...Why? Wouldn't it make you happy if there was a girl like that?" she asked.

"Whether I would be happy or not doesn't make a difference... There are no emotions that last forever," Minoru replied, looking down at the table. "Eventually there would be something to make that girl hate me; she might even grow to despise me so much she would want to kill me. That always remains a possibility, so it's better to not have a relationship at all."

For a while both were silent. Minoru didn't look up and kept staring down at the table. He didn't want to be even having this conversation. As soon as he was alone again, thinking back to this moment, he was sure that he would regret every word he said.

Finally, Yumiko broke the silence with a stern voice.

"Hmph. I see. In other words you just don't want to be hated. You want everyone to like you," she said.

"...That's not what I said. I only want them to be apathetic to me. That's all," Minoru replied, shaking his head without looking up, but Yumiko didn't stop there.

"If you're hated, all you have to do is ignore it. No matter who you are, there's going to be at least one person out there who hates you, and I'm no different," she said.

Minoru slowly lifted his gaze and looked at Yumiko across the table.

She had straight, flowing glossy hair. It didn't seem as if she was wearing any makeup, with her skin as white as magnolias. Her eyelashes were thick and her eyes cool and filled with light.

Taking his eyes again off of the girl who ten out of ten would call beautiful, Minoru muttered, "Are you sure you know what it's really like to be hated? Do you really think you know?"

But whatever Yumiko's answer was, it did not reach Minoru's ears.

Before her pink lips could move to form that answer, the elevator doors at the north end of the room groaned as they reluctantly opened. The young man wearing a cap who leaped out of the elevator was someone Minoru was familiar with. He was one of the Jet Eyes, DD, code name "Searcher," and as soon as he entered the room, he called out in a loud voice.

"E-everyone! It's him! He's returned! The one responsible for the murder in Ikebukuro is Igniter!"

With a loud thud, Yumiko slammed her mug on the table.

Once again, everyone gathered in one place. At the west end of the room, there was a space where folding chairs set in front of a large eighty- or so inch monitor that looked like it was used for meetings.

Riri, who stepped in front of Yumiko, DD, and Minoru

after they had taken their seats, lightly tapped on the monitor with a stick pointer. The 8K monitor flicked on and displayed a single photograph. The photograph, captioned by the title "Identified Ruby Eye Host No. 19: Igniter," was very blurry and taken from diagonally behind the subject. All that one could tell from the photograph was that it was a thin man in a suit.

As Riri turned around, she had a stern look on her young face.

"...It appears that, unfortunately, Igniter is alive and well," she said.

"I expected as much," replied Yumiko in a low voice. "A Ruby Eye isn't so weak as to die from being stabbed in the stomach with a knife. Next time, I won't miss his heart, I assure you."

When Minoru turned to glance at Yumiko, her face was more tense than he had ever seen it before, and it wasn't just Yumiko. DD, who was sitting next to him, also looked nervous.

From Minoru's perspective, Igniter was the second Ruby Eye he'd heard of after Biter. From his code name, it seemed that his power had something to do with fire, but was he really that dangerous of an opponent?

Riri, who seemed to read his mind, said, "First of all, for Mikkun's sake, let's go over what we already know," and turned back around to control the monitor with her pointer.

"Mikkun, huh?" said DD to Minoru's left. When his eyes met Minoru's, he made a faint, sympathetic smile.

"Well, it's still more of a proper nickname than 'DD.' I mean Oli-V even calls me 'D&D,'" DD continued.

Minoru found himself smiling and asked, "Professor decided your nickname as well, right? What is it based on?"

Before DD could answer, Yumiko, who was sitting farther away, replied, "It's just an acronym of his real name, Denjirou Daimon."

Denjirou Daimon, huh? thought Minoru.

Yumiko, who had stolen DD's answer away from him, ignored his frown and asked, "Where is Oli-V anyway?"

"He's scouting out Ikebukuro, just in case," DD replied.

"Is there any chance that Igniter will return to the scene of the crime?" Yumiko asked.

"Well, he is like an arsonist in a way, but I can't say for sure…," DD replied.

"You there, stop your chitchatting," scolded Riri, like a teacher, as she turned back around. Yumiko, DD, and Minoru all straightened their posture.

On the monitor a number of new photographs were displayed. Their resolution was low, as if they had been taken from security camera footage, and all showed nothing but something burning on the street at night.

"Like his code name suggests, Igniter manipulates flame. Do you remember seeing a number of incidents in the news in October about people whose faces were severely burned when their cigarettes suddenly burst into flame?" asked Riri.

Minoru nodded in an ambiguous way. "…I have a feeling I read something about it in the paper."

"All of those incidents were the work of Igniter. In the beginning, we hypothesized that his power was to heat objects by amplifying the vibrations in the atoms of those objects. His code name is also based on that hypothesis, but we were wrong. He is technically not an 'igniter,' but a 'combustion catalyzer.'"

"A 'combustion catalyzer'? Just what does his power manipulate?" Minoru asked.

"It's oxygen," answered Riri gravely. "Igniter has the power to manipulate oxygen molecules in the air and concentrate them at a single point. Our misunderstanding of the situation led to us having to pay a terrible price."

"A terrible price…," repeated Minoru.

"We'll talk about that later…once you've gone to meet her. DD, can you show us that picture taken today at the scene of the crime?"

DD, the Searcher, nodded, taking a smartphone out of his tactical jacket. Riri took the data he sent and displayed it on the monitor.

Seeing the first photograph, Minoru gasped.

DD must have taken the photo with a long telescopic lens. In comparison to the previous pictures, this photograph was very clear. It seemed to have been taken from a high place, looking down at a brick walkway. One area of the bricks was whitened as if they had been bleached by the sun, and in the very center of that area was a pitch-black stain. The stain was distinctly in the form of a person, and it was clear what had happened. Here a person had been engulfed in flame.

"He's becoming a lot more powerful, isn't he?" remarked Yumiko.

DD nodded before giving his explanation. "Today, at around three thirty in the afternoon, in the street of a shopping district near the west exit of Ikebukuro Station, a twenty-five-year-old businessman suddenly was covered in flame and burned to death. At the same time, I sensed by smell that a Ruby Eye's powers were being activated and quickly went to the scene with Oli-V, but by the time we arrived, everything was over."

At the words "around three thirty," Minoru's body tensed. Around that time, Minoru was with Yumiko in that taxi on the highway, and Ikebukuro Station wasn't very far from the route that they took to get here. In a place that Minoru might have been able to see out that taxi window, a Ruby Eye had been making a kill.

Seeing Minoru's shock, Riri said, "Mikkun, you shouldn't be so hard on yourself. Although it depends on a number of factors, Jet Eyes who don't have a power like DD's usually can't smell a Ruby Eye's power more than one hundred meters away."

"...Okay..." Minoru nodded, and DD continued his explanation.

"According to the testimony of witnesses gathered by the Ikebukuro police, the source of the flame was, like before, a lighter, but this time the flame didn't dissipate until the victim's body had completely carbonized. Additionally, people up to twenty meters away felt a wind rushing to the source of the flame. There were nine people taken to the hospital who had fainted after suffering from oxygen deprivation."

"Yes, that itself is the most dangerous element of Igniter's power," said Riri gravely, writing on the monitor with her pointer.

Over the black stain, it said, "Combustion Catalyzation = Oxygen Deprivation." Despite everything else, her handwriting was a bit childish.

"Due to his ability to manipulate the oxygen in the atmosphere at will, Igniter has two forms of attack. One is to concentrate oxygen around a source of flame, to explosively catalyze combustion. The other is to, for a limited time, deprive a certain area of oxygen," explained Riri, turning around to look at Yumiko, DD, and Minoru in turn.

"Of the two, the most dangerous is the oxygen deprivation attack. That's because while the combustion attack is flashy, it requires a very important initial condition. Mikkun, can you tell me what that is?" Riri asked.

Suddenly asked a question, Minoru, feeling as if he was in the middle of an afternoon class, raised his hand to answer. "Y-yes. Is it that a spark, or initial flame, is required?"

"Precisely! Igniter's power can concentrate oxygen around a certain point, but he cannot start the fire. Therefore, either he must use an existing flame, such as a lit cigarette, a burning stick of incense, or a gas stove, or he must supply the flame himself with a lighter or something. For Third Eye hosts such as yourselves, who have very fast reaction times, it is not that difficult to avoid a combustion attack. However, an oxygen deprivation attack is a different matter. Even if you want to avoid it, it's not something that you can see," Riri explained.

Riri then spread her arms wide, as if she were following a radio exercise routine, and took a deep breath.

"When you are fighting, your bodies, stimulated by their Third Eyes, exhaust a large amount of oxygen. Your breathing becomes faster and deeper. If you take a full breath in an oxygen-deprived environment, it is even possible that you will immediately faint on the spot," Riri said gravely, as if she were describing something that had already happened before.

But after immediately wiping that expression from her face, she stuck her right hand in her lab coat pocket, digging around for something.

"So the next time you face Igniter in combat, I will have you use these," Riri said, showing them small gas cylinders about fifteen centimeters in length. Attached to the cylinders were clear hoses and a small mouthpiece.

"These are specially modified forms of the small compressed gas cylinders that the Japan Self-Defence Forces's marine units use. It is possible to breathe using just these cylinders for a maximum of five minutes. I have modified them so that you can equip them under your clothes and extend the hose from the cylinder up to your necks. The cylinders are filled with enriched air, containing a high concentration of oxygen," explained Riri.

Just then, DD raised his hand. "So if we have those cylinders, we don't have to worry about the breathing problem. That's our Professor! But rather than those small cylinders, wouldn't it be better for us to use full-size scuba tanks? For people like us, the weight would mean nothing."

"That brings us to another problem. Can you guess why I made these cylinders small and had them equipped with thin, clear hoses?" Riri asked.

There was silence.

For at least about five seconds until Minoru slowly raised his hand.

"Oh, go right ahead Mikkun," said Riri.

"Umm...well," said Minoru in a small voice, shrinking away. "Igniter is able to manipulate oxygen, right? Therefore, if he realized that we had cylinders of compressed oxygen, wouldn't he also be able to manipulate the oxygen in those containers?"

"Correct!" shouted Riri.

DD and Yumiko clapped in admiration. Riri smiled, and with her slippers flip-flipping, she ran over and took something out of her left coat pocket. Minoru reflexively extended his hand to Riri's outstretched fist, and she dropped a piece of nostalgic-looking strawberry milk candy into his palm.

"That was some nice insight. Good job," she said with a smile. Riri then ran back to the monitor, and when she had turned around, she looked again like a stern teacher.

"That is precisely the case. The gas cylinders are pressurized to two hundred fifty atmospheres. Just think about what the enemy could do with that. He could send it flying in an instant at best or make it explode at worst. You all wouldn't get by with just a scratch. Therefore, you need to hide the small cylinder under your clothes and stealthily breathe from the tube at your neck. If the cylinders are discovered, you will have to discard them immediately. If it comes to that... Well, you'll have to manage on fighting spirit."

"It won't be a problem," Yumiko said in a low, tense voice. "As long as I can get close to him once, I'll make sure to finish him."

Minoru felt that the temperature in the room dropped a few degrees.

Wasn't the SFD's stated goal in dealing with Ruby Eyes to capture them and surgically remove their Third Eye? It sounded as if Yumiko was declaring that she would kill him, regardless of the circumstances.

Riri, sensing Minoru's confusion, sighed before continuing. "We'll discuss the tactical details of the operation after Oli-V returns. For the time being, having confirmed that Igniter has returned to the city and that his power has increased by a large margin, I will bring this meeting to a close. I'm sorry, Yukko, but could you take Mikkun to see her?"

"..."

The black-haired Accelerator bit her lip and looked down. After a short pause, she stood up and turned to Minoru. "All right. Minoru, come with me."

Following Yumiko out of the elevator, Minoru looked at his surroundings. Unlike the fifth floor, which had all of the interior walls taken out to make one large room, the fourth floor, one floor below it, was just like a regular apartment floor, with nothing particularly strange about it. A concrete-lined hall connecting the apartments extended from left to right, and there were two doors on either side.

Chasing after Yumiko, who had started down the hall making quiet sounds with the heels of her sneakers, he finally arrived at the eastern-most door with her.

While waiting for the door to be unlocked, Minoru looked at the nameplate. Underneath the room number, 404, was a very properly written set of names, AZU–IKOMA. Azu was Yumiko's surname, so perhaps that meant that she lived here with someone named Ikoma.

Ignoring Minoru's questioning gaze with her back to him, Yumiko turned the doorknob. From the other side of the opened door came a sweet scent, which immediately gave away that this was where a woman or women lived. When

Minoru occasionally went to clean Norie's room, it had this same kind of smell.

Minoru, unable to bear the silence any longer, asked softly, "Is this your room?"

"Yes," Yumiko answered briefly without turning around before she entered the room.

With no other choice, Minoru quietly entered the room after muttering, "Sorry to intrude."

Again, unlike the fifth floor, this room was relatively normal. From the step up into the apartment, the hallway stretched forward, and to the left and right were two sliding doors and one swinging door. At the end of the hall was a glass door that appeared to lead into the living room. The layout appeared to be a standard arrangement of a two-bedroom apartment with living room, kitchen, and dining room.

After removing her shoes at the door and stepping up into the hallway, Yumiko finally turned around and glared at Minoru. "If you enter the far door on the right, I'll throw you off the veranda. ...You can use those slippers over there."

"Th-thanks...," Minoru replied.

"Follow me," continued Yumiko.

Yumiko, who turned back around, walked straight to the glass door at the end of the hall, turned the knob, and pushed it open. From the darkness on the other side of the door, which clicked open, the sweet smell grew stronger. It wasn't an artificial smell, but a refreshing scent of real flowers. Along with it, he thought faintly, was also the sense that there was a person there as well.

Naturally softening his footsteps as he entered the living room, he noticed that while the lights were off, the apartment was not cold—perhaps the thermostat had been left up. Because of the Third Eye in his chest, Minoru's eyes quickly adjusted to the darkness, and the faint light of the city coming through the window was enough for him to see around the room.

In the twelve tatami mat–size living-dining area, there was a sofa and TV, but no other large furniture. Instead, there was a large bed in the center of the room. Furthermore, it appeared to be a hospital bed with functions to raise and lower it.

Around the bed were several flowers. There were lilies and heather and jasmine, as well as other flowers that Minoru did not know the names of, and they all spread out their pure white flower petals, shining faintly in the darkness.

Urged on by Yumiko, Minoru moved to the side of the bed. Sleeping there was a girl who looked to be the same age as him. Her brown hair was cut short like a boy's, but the reason Minoru was sure she was a girl was that her figure was overwhelmingly delicate. Her skin, as white as the flowers surrounding her, looked as if it would melt away in sunlight. Her long eyelashes were closed and unmoving, but from her slightly opened lips, a person could hear her faintly breathing.

It took a few seconds for Minoru to realize for sure that she wasn't simply asleep. From under the bed ran a clear tube and black cord connected to a machine on the other side of the bed. A monitor partially hidden by the flowers showed an unusually low heart rate and body temperature. This girl was not sleeping, but in a coma.

After slowly breathing in the air scented by the flowers, Minoru turned to Yumiko.

"Is this…Ms. Ikoma?" he asked.

"Yes. This is Sanae Ikoma. Until last month, we worked together as a team. Her code name is 'Shooter,'" Yumiko answered.

Minoru blinked twice at the fact that the name didn't seem to match the faint presence of the girl in front of him. Yumiko, without lifting her gaze from the girl in front of her, continued.

"She was an archer. As long as it was a target that she could see, she had the power to hit her target every time, even if she was shooting from ten kilometers away. Sanae and I worked together in a perfect team of a forward and backup. In the month after the SFD was formed, we captured seven Ruby Eyes. With my stun baton and Sanae's tranquilizing arrows, there was not a single Ruby Eye who could escape us. Until that one man, Igniter, showed up...," Yumiko explained, her last sentence trailing off into a subdued sigh, and then sat down on a corner of the bed.

Yumiko twisted around and brushed her left hand through Sanae's short hair, and then continued her explanation in a whisper. "...We, who firmly believed that Igniter's power was to heat a target, thought that we would be safe as long as he didn't see us. So we planned to chase him in a car that had a heat-resistant ceramic coating and have Sanae shoot at him from inside the car. However, that man's true power was to concentrate oxygen in a single spot. Even though we were facing an opponent like that, we had taken the worst strategy by shutting ourselves in a closed room."

As if she was remembering what happened at the time, Yumiko suddenly took a deep breath.

"...Igniter took away all of the oxygen in the car, and DD who was driving, myself in the passenger's seat, and Sanae in the backseat all breathed in a lungful of oxygen-deprived air. I was somehow able to open the door, grab DD, and escape with my accelerator power, but my consciousness was fading, and with the last ounce of power, I leaped once more and stabbed Igniter with a knife and immediately lost consciousness. By the time I came to, Igniter had disappeared, leaving only a bloodstain. While I and DD were able to get away with just fainting for a few minutes, Sanae, who was left in the car, suffered irreversible brain damage."

Minoru realized that at some point he had held his breath and stopped breathing. Taking in a deep breath, he tried to imagine what it would be like to breathe in oxygen-deprived air, but it was beyond him.

On the other hand, Yumiko had leaned forward and wrapped her arms around Sanae's sleeping head.

"Sanae actually shouldn't be able to breathe on her own anymore. From her cerebellum to her brain stem, everything has irreversibly stopped functioning. However, as you can see, it only looks like she's just sleeping. ...Do you understand why?" Yumiko asked.

"...No," Minoru replied.

"It's because of the Third Eye," Yumiko answered. "The Third Eye in Sanae's right shoulder has taken over her central nervous system and is making her continue to breathe. You saw what happened four days ago, right, Utsugi? Biter's brain was blown away, but he still kept thrashing about."

"She's gone...berserk?" Minoru asked in a raspy voice.

Yumiko nodded slightly. "Yes, right now, Sanae is quietly going berserk. Even though her real consciousness no longer exists, her Third Eye is not letting her die. It's awful...isn't it? Chief Himi and Professor Isa both say that we should surgically remove her Third Eye. Remove it and let her die a proper death, and then return her to her family. But... But I..." Yumiko trailed off, her words containing a pain Minoru had yet to hear from her that rang through the space of the room buried in flowers.

"I don't want to forget her," Yumiko continued. "I don't want to make Sanae part of the past. I want to make more day-to-day memories with her...even if it's just memories of me talking to her as she is now, unable to wake up."

Minoru realized that Yumiko's words described the exact opposite of what Minoru's wish was. Was that why? Was that why Yumiko was so against Minoru's wish of wanting everyone to forget about him?

However, he wasn't able to put his conjecture or

anything else into words. He was overwhelmed by the situation, overwhelmed by the cruel reality that occurs because of Ruby Eyes and Jet Eyes fighting each other. That a small, kind-looking girl like this could lose her life like this, in just a single battle...

"...Why?" Minoru finally asked, even though it was way past the time to ask. "Why didn't you or Sanae choose to have your Third Eyes removed and forget everything?"

"If I had known this would have happened, I might have done that," Yumiko replied.

Yumiko's answer itself was not combative, but her eyes as they gazed down in the darkness looked as if they had cold flames within them.

"But I will not run away anymore. For Sanae's sake, I cannot run away anymore. Until I finish with Igniter, until I finish disposing of every single one of the Ruby Eyes," she said.

Dispose of. In other words, have their Third Eyes surgically removed or kill the host. Yumiko's determination was admirable, but at the same time, Minoru couldn't help but think that something about it was wrong.

It was true that those who host a red Third Eye are dangerous. Even though they look no different from everybody else, their psyche is filled with the desire to kill others, and they have been gifted with special powers. The only ones who can sense their presence are other Third Eye hosts, so it makes sense that it is necessary to have an organization such as the SFD with which to oppose them.

However, there was no reason for Yumiko or Sanae, both of whom must have been normal girls before they became Jet Eyes, to fight them directly. There must be other options.

For example, if Yumiko and company were to assist in finding and tracking the Ruby Eyes, the police or the Japan Self-Defense Forces should be able to do the rest. Ruby Eyes weren't immortal. If something like a tranquilizer dart would work, then that is all the more reason to not get directly involved. Was it really necessary for Yumiko and company to put their lives in danger to fight?

However, Minoru wasn't able to voice that doubt. The fact that Sanae was laying there asleep, never to wake again, was proof that things had already gone past the point of no return. What finally broke the silence was Yumiko's voice, which had regained its calm.

"...You'll have to participate in the battle with Igniter now that he has regained his strength. I don't think you will be fighting directly. However, you should prepare yourself just in case. From now on, even if you get caught up in a battle, you shouldn't fight without a plan...not like what happened with Biter. We will proactively seek out the Ruby Eyes, neutralize and dispose of them. You mustn't forget that you are now part of the hunt."

After Yumiko finished her declaration, she stood up from the bed and pointed toward the door.

"We've prepared room 403 for you to stay in," she said, adding, "though there's nothing but a bed."

Following Yumiko as she headed for the door, Minoru finally asked the question that had been bugging him since before they entered the room.

"Do you live here, Yumiko?" he asked.

"Yes. I commute to school from here. That is, when I feel like going," Yumiko replied.

"...What kind of explanation did you give your parents?" Minoru asked in return.

"I told them that I'm attending a boarding school. The real reason my parents believed me was due to Chief Himi's reputation, his virtuous nature, and his power, though," replied Yumiko.

In other words, she had her family's memories altered.

Did she really have to go that far? Minoru thought, surprised, feeling the weight of the fact that the current situation was dire enough to lead her to do such a thing.

As Minoru prepared to leave the room, just as he set his foot out into the hallway, he felt as if someone had called him and turned around, but of course there was no change in the silhouette of the girl as she slept on the bed.

5

When his cell phone rang, Ayato Suka was just preparing to go to sleep.

It wasn't the phone that he was using for work. It was a smartphone he had signed a new contract for two months ago, and there was only one person he had exchanged that number with.

It was one of *them*.

As Suka reached for his cell phone, he took a deep breath, sending oxygen to his brain. When meeting with "them," even over the phone, he had to be very cautious. With his brain clear and ready, he pressed the button to answer the phone.

"Good evening, Mr. Igniter."

On the other end of the phone was a woman's voice, which rang as smooth as silk. Like before, Suka still couldn't even guess what age she was.

"…I told you to stop calling me by that name," Suka argued. The ones who gave him that wrongheaded name, "Igniter," were his enemies, the black hunters. But the woman on the phone just laughed.

"A name is nothing but a code. It doesn't help to have more than one. Even I put up with the nickname forced on me by my superiors."

"…Well, that's your choice to make, Ms. Liquidizer. …Why are you calling me at this hour?" asked Suka.

"I'm just checking in on you. Welcome back, Mr. Igniter. It looks like going off to train in the mountains paid off for you. That show you put on for us today was wonderful," Liquidizer replied.

"…Hmph," Suka muttered, thinking, *You say that as if you saw it yourself*, but swallowing those words before they made it out of his mouth. If he said something like that, this woman would only reply with something like, "But of course."

The woman didn't seem to take offense to Suka's attitude and kept talking in her smooth voice.

"Your power is absolutely wonderful. With that much potential, you would easily qualify to become a member of our organization, Mr. Igniter. …So what do you think? Are you still not ready to join us?"

"No, I am not," Suka replied, holding back his irritation. "You all may be like me, but we don't share the same goals. Not at all. Despite being given powers and an obligation to a cause, none of you act on it. You all just gather together in some hole, thinking only of protecting yourselves."

"Oh, so you are saying that we Ruby Eyes should just go out and slaughter humans as much as we can, until we are hunted and killed by the Jet Eyes? Just like that handsome, sad, stupid gourmet, Biter?" Ms. Liquidizer asked.

"…He died?" asked Suka.

"Yes, four days ago," replied the woman.

Suka said a silent prayer for Biter, whom he had never met nor spoken to. Biter hadn't known about Suka, nor should he have known about the existence of any other Ruby Eye, but to Suka, they were one of the same mind.

Opening his eyes, Suka spoke in harsher tones than before. "I don't like your attitude. At the very least Biter was a martyr

to our cause. Furthermore, aren't you partially at fault for his death, for deciding that you didn't need to approach him?"

"We had no need for an inelegant power like his," Liquidizer replied with a chuckle. "But you are different, Mr. Igniter. Your power is beautiful. Our doors are always open to you. If you ever change your mind, just give us a call."

"...Hmph," muttered Suka as he moved to end the call. But just before he could, some unsettling words reached his ears.

"Be careful. The black ones have already started to move. This time they are determined to catch... No, they are determined to kill you," Liquidizer said before ending the call from her end.

Suka stared at his phone for a minute before returning it to its charging stand.

"...I'm the one who's going to be doing the hunting, Ms. Liquidizer," he muttered.

6

Minoru, who didn't sleep well on his brand-new bed in its unfamiliar room, left SFD Headquarters at 6:00 a.m. so that he could return to his home in Saitama. The one who saw him off at the exit of the wooded area around the apartment complex, in the freezing cold, was DD, whom Minoru hardly had a chance to speak with the previous night.

"Sorry it's just me, but the others tend to stay up late and never get up in the morning," DD said.

"Don't worry about it...," Minoru said, smiling a little as he remembered the (no-alcohol) welcome party thrown for him in the large fifth-floor room that lasted late into the night. Then, after hesitating a few seconds, Minoru turned to ask DD something that had been bothering him for a while.

"...Do all of the SFD members live in that apartment building?" he asked.

"Yeah. The eight rooms on the third and fourth floors are used for our private residences," DD answered.

"Eight rooms...," Minoru repeated, thinking back over the names of the members he knew.

On the fourth floor, room 404 was Yumiko and Sanae's room. The neighboring room 403 was for Minoru to use. There was also Professor Riri; DD; Oli-V, who didn't return that night; and the mysterious "Lindenberger." It didn't seem that Chief Himi lived at headquarters, so that left two additional rooms.

As if he had read Minoru's thoughts, DD nodded. "There are also some members you probably haven't been introduced to yet... I mean, I'm not sure you even can be introduced to one of them..."

"Huh? What do you mean by that?" asked Minoru.

"It has to do with her power. I mean, even I haven't seen her face in the two months I've been here. Maybe you'll be able to meet her if you're lucky."

"Well...okay." That wasn't exactly a clear explanation, but Minoru didn't have much time so he decided to worry about that later. Instead, he asked the question he had been wanting to ask most.

"So... How is everyone explaining this to their parents?"

"Oh...that," DD, Denjirou Daimon, replied, pulling at the brim of his trademark cap. "Well, it's sort of done on a case-by-case basis, but basically we have the chief do a little memory manipulation."

Everyone had that done?! thought Minoru, surprised. But DD quickly waved his head back and forth as if to say, "It's not what you think."

"It's not like we made them forget we exist or something," DD explained. "Yumiko and Oli-V have it so everyone thinks they're at a boarding school, and for me, it's that I'm in a study abroad program in France for the culinary arts. No one plans to return home until everything has been taken care of here. ...To be honest, I wasn't planning on saying this yet, but Utsugi, I think that you should do the same."

Minoru immediately knew why DD was telling him this. It was dangerous.

If your identity was exposed to the Ruby Eyes, it was not unlikely that your family would be attacked. Actually, Minoru's adoptive sister, Norie, was attacked by Biter and kidnapped. Though she got away unscathed in the end, she could have easily suffered a grave injury or—and he didn't even want to think about this—she could have been killed.

When put that way, it would certainly give him peace of mind to take DD up on his offer.

However, at the same time, it would put an end to the "ever-repeating daily life" that Minoru sought. His routine that took him back and forth from his home and school and the library would disappear, and he would be subject to a large number of new memories. Minoru didn't think he could handle that.

All of the memories that Minoru had would flow deep into his brain and attempt to connect with that one incident. Once the switch was flipped, Minoru would be forced to relive that memory. The memory of that terrible incident, which took the lives of his kind parents and his beloved older sister Wakaba.

Already, at that very moment, Minoru found it hard to breathe. Both of his arms went cold and numb, and his sense of balance began to suffer. His vision tilted, and a dusty smell filled his nose as he remembered that dark, cramped storage compartment under the floor. *Thump, thump, thump* went the sound of violent footsteps, closing in. Minoru could feel his heart rapidly beating, like an alarm bell. Or maybe it wasn't his heart that was beating, but that parasitic black eye that fed on the wounds of human hearts...

"...tsugi. Utsugi, can you hear me?"

His right shoulder shaken, Minoru suddenly looked up. In front of him was DD, who looked confused and suspicious.

"Are you all right, man?" he asked.

"Uh... Yeah, I'm fine. It's nothing," said Minoru quickly and a bit frantically, shaking his head as he took one step back. He readjusted his messenger bag, which contained the small canister Riri gave him.

"I guess I should get going now. If you call or text me, I'll come running as fast as I can... I'll consider what you said about moving in," Minoru said.

"Yeah, please do. Also, make sure you stay alert in case you catch the scent of a Ruby Eye. Even I can't sniff them out if they're in a place as far away as Saitama," said DD, who seemed sincerely worried.

"I'll be careful. Tell everyone I wish them well. ...I'll see you later," said Minoru, waving back at DD before raising his scarf to his mouth and walking down the path out of the wooded area around the apartment complex.

When Minoru went through the rusted gates that led out into the adjacent two-lane street, a middle school student in a tracksuit who was just crossing by looked suspiciously at Minoru. If due to Chief Himi's barrier, outsiders really couldn't perceive the path leading to SFD Headquarters, it must have looked as if Minoru had suddenly sprung out from under the trees.

Using the map on his smartphone, Minoru walked to the Tokyo Metro West Waseda Station and took the Fukutoshin line to Ikebukuro, where he switched over to an express train on the JR Saikyou line. As it was early Saturday morning, the train was fairly empty, and after dozing off for a while, Minoru arrived at Yonohonmachi Station, which was the closest to his house.

For the nearly two kilometers between the station and his

house, Minoru took off his coat and scarf and did some light jogging. Compared to his usual daily routine, it was only one-fifth of the distance, but he told himself that was enough for today, and so he did a light cooldown routine in front of his house.

Minoru glanced at his watch as he stretched his legs. It was exactly one hour since he had left headquarters. Given the fact that he had waited a while at Ikebukuro Station for the express train, he was surprised he had gotten home so quickly, but all the same, it would be hard for him to immediately respond if he got a message that a Ruby Eye had appeared.

If I really want to be serious about fighting alongside the members of the SFD, I really should think about moving in to headquarters, but still..., Minoru thought indecisively to himself as he finished his stretches and picked up his bag and coat.

Minoru's adoptive sister, Norie, was probably still asleep, so he had to make sure not to make a sound when he opened the door and went into the house. But before he unlocked that brand-new door that had just been replaced, he breathed in the cold air deeply through his nose and concentrated his thoughts on what he could smell.

Minoru couldn't smell that characteristic violent, animalistic scent that gave away the presence of a Ruby Eye, but that wasn't enough to guarantee that everything was safe. A Ruby Eye's scent could only be detected when their power is being activated. As long as Minoru lived in this house, there would never be zero risk.

I know, I know, but..., thought Minoru, swallowing a sigh. He then turned the key to unlock the door and entered the house.

As soon as he did, the sound of slippers hitting the floor suddenly came close, and in the next moment, Minoru found himself tightly bound.

"Welcome back! Mii!"

"Uwah, w-wait a second, Norie!" Minoru replied as he struggled to escape from her embrace, but his adoptive sister, Norie, wouldn't let him go.

"I-I'm home… But what's the matter?" asked Minoru.

"Don't you know?" Norie replied.

Norie, a thirty-one-year-old who worked at the prefectural office as an assistant supervisor, the spitting image of a hardworking career woman, had an expression on her face that could only be described as depressed.

"This house is too big for just one person…," she said.

"Too big for one person…? Aren't I always telling you that you should go ahead and start looking for a husband without waiting for me to graduate?" Minoru replied.

"There you go saying those things again…," Norie said, puffing her cheeks as Minoru finally was able to escape from her embrace, before going on to say something absolutely outrageous. "I mean, since we've come this far, I guess I should just go ahead and wait two years and marry you!"

Thump! Minoru stubbed his right toe on the step up into the hall and shook his head back and forth as he writhed in pain. "Wh-what are you saying?! Two years? I-I'm still a high school student and…even though we're cousins five degrees removed, it's against the law to marry someone of the same family they're adopted into!"

"What…? Really?"

"Really!" Minoru said. Actually, it wasn't necessarily against the law for the child of a legal guardian and an adopted child to get married, but Minoru didn't plan on telling her that. Before Norie could say something like, "Well, we can just unadopt you first!" Minoru put his hands on her shoulders and turned her around to face the kitchen.

"…Anyway, I smell something odd coming from the kitchen," said Minoru.

"Huh? Ah! No! The fish!" Norie said, running off.

When she finds a husband, it had better be someone who can keep tabs on her, thought Minoru as he chased after Norie.

7

Glug.

Glug, glug.

The source of the loud sound was coming from my throat and lungs.

It was the sound of precious air, precious oxygen being pushed out and being replaced with water.

When water flows down your esophagus and into your stomach, it serves a purpose vital to life. In that role it is nothing other than "the water of life," but in this case, when it flows into your lungs through your bronchial tubes, it becomes a lethal poison. What a fickle thing.

Ah, but really... This is incredibly painful. If I knew it was going to be like this, I would have chosen a different method. I could have used charcoal or hydrogen sulfide... There were many other things I could have tried. But to be absolutely sure, this really was the only way.

This locked car, drifting on its way to the bottom of the water, was nothing short of a death chamber. Already, the two other passengers have stopped moving, just seconds ago. All that is left is for me to follow them. Then everything will be over. I will be free, and yet...

Why is my left hand struggling desperately to undo my seat belt?

Why is my right hand using my beloved Montblanc pen to try and break the window?

Why is my freed body trying to slip out of the car through the broken window...?

I am going to die. I already decided that I have no other options when I floored the pedal. I ignored the pleas from the passenger's seat and the screams from the backseat and flung us into the dark sea.

Yet here I am, swimming desperately with both my arms and legs.

I can see the gray surface of the water. I will soon have returned. To that world of life, filled with sweet air...

Air.

Oxygen.

I want to breathe.

But now my arms and legs have stopped moving, and I begin to sink again.

No...

I want to live.

I want to live. I want to live, I want to live, I want to live! Even though it makes me a coward, a traitor... No matter how much I might regret it in the end...

With the last ounce of my strength, I kick the water.

My outstretched hand breaks through the surface of the water, countless oxygen molecules gently caressing it.

I want to breathe. I want to breathe. I want to breathe, I want to breathe, I want to breathe. But I just can't seem to get my head above water.

But at that moment, through the wavering surface of the water, I see a strange red light falling down toward me, and in my right hand, I grasp it.

I feel a terrible, burning pain.

"...Aaaahhh!!!!!!" Ayato Suka screamed as he leaped up violently.

"Gah... Gah... Gah..." went the sound of his throat as he sucked in large quantities of air. As he breathed, with both hands he gathered oxygen around his mouth, as if he were eating it.

When Suka came to a few seconds later, he realized that he was not underwater, but in his bed.

It was the dream Suka always had. Wiping the sweat from his forehead with the sleeve of his pajamas, he let out a deep sigh. Even though it had already been three months since then, he had seen that dream as often as he did when he first saw it. Once every three days he was sure to have that nightmare.

It certainly was a frightening dream to have, but...surely this was part of the process, he thought. He had these nightmares so that he would always remember his obligation, his obligation to renew his hatred and disdain of the garbage that would not understand the preciousness of oxygen.

Of course, his is a necessary pain, Suka thought, *and the deaths of those two, they were a necessary sacrifice.*

Once Suka confirmed that his breathing had returned to normal, he got up out of his futon bed, neatly folded the mattress layer and cover, and put them away in his closet. He washed his face, brushed his teeth, and got to work moving plants from his living room and out onto the veranda. As he worked, he looked at the large map he had put up on the wall.

On Monday of next week, he wanted to burn at least one, if possible two more pieces of human garbage, so that he could draw a beautiful symbol in the middle of this polluted city.

"Oxygen... Oxygen...," sang Suka, having already forgotten about his nightmare as he went about his work.

8

Saturday and Sunday passed by peacefully without event.

Minoru didn't sense the smell of a Ruby Eye, and he didn't receive any calls from Yumiko, either. The only time Minoru went outside was to do his morning running routine, and inside he did things like help Norie, watch movies with her, and of course study.

On Monday, December 16, the sky was overcast since morning.

When Minoru had finished his morning classes, he, like always, went alone toward the cafeteria. The sky that he could see from the hallway looked heavy, as if it might snow at any moment, but the expressions of all of the students around were bright. The end of semester, midterm exams were over, and there was only one week until Christmas and winter break, so an excitement characteristic of this time enveloped all of the students.

Minoru had visited that strange apartment building in Shinjuku and had become a member of the Jet Eye team that fights against Ruby Eyes just three days before. But after having returned to his daily routine, Minoru felt that all of the things he experienced in that place had quickly lost their realism.

I'll need to buy a present for Norie soon, but it feels kind of wrong to buy a present for someone out of an allowance you've received from that person, doesn't it? If she could just let me get a part-time job..., thought Minoru as he lined up in front of the cafeteria meal-ticket machine.

"Oh, hey, Utsugi."

Just then, Minoru was called from behind, and after freezing up a moment, he slowly turned around.

The person standing there was of course not a Ruby Eye, but a male student wearing the same uniform as Minoru. After all, he was at school, in the cafeteria of Saitama Prefectural Yoshiki High School. But at the same time this wasn't someone that Minoru had expected. It was Oguu, a first-year student from Class Eight who was also a member of the track club.

A week ago, together with two upperclassmen from the

track club, he had called Minoru out behind the school's dojo to beat him up. As Minoru was thinking about how he should react to being called out by someone like that, Oguu changed his expression from the intrepid look of an athlete to a bit of an awkwardly ironic smile.

"You don't have to get all worried like that. I'm not going to pull any of that crap anymore," he said.

"...Is that right?"

"Do you always eat in the cafeteria?" asked Oguu.

"Well, usually. What about yourself?"

"Same here. And you don't have to be so polite, man," said Oguu.

"Umm... Okay," said Minoru, taken aback.

By the time their conversation reached that point, they had already made it to the front of the line, and after a little bit of thought, Minoru pushed the button for a Meat Udon Set. Before he got his Third Eye, Minoru had been fine with just the udon, but ever since he was infected by it, his metabolism seemed to have gone up, and without the two Inari sushi that came with the set, he wouldn't be able to last until dinner.

After paying with his IC card and taking the ticket, Minoru quickly turned to go to the food counter, but...

"I'm surprised that's enough food for you."

...Minoru was called from behind again and lost his chance to escape.

"...Well, I'm not in any clubs, after all," said Minoru to Oguu, as Oguu slipped a thousand-yen note into the machine and ordered tickets for a Chicken Nanban Set, as well as a large bowl of rice and croquettes. After he grabbed his three meal tickets and change, he immediately walked over to join Minoru.

They continued to have a strange conversation after that as

they picked up their trays from the food counter and moved to an empty table to sit across from each other. After Minoru took one sip of his udon while Oguu started to wolf down his food, he set his determination and ventured into delicate territory.

"Umm... Oguu? Is Minowa doing well?" he asked.

Oguu furrowed his brow, shaved so that it was just barely within school rules, and froze with his chopsticks held in mid-air. The sweet sauce from his chicken dripped onto his plate. But the way he furrowed his brow and frowned was apparently not an expression of anger.

"Well... I mean... Sure, she's doing well. Ever since she returned to school she's been practicing with her club like usual," Oguu answered and then opened his mouth wide and stuffed the chicken into his mouth.

Tomomi Minowa, who was in the same class as Oguu and a track club member, had been attacked by Biter ten days earlier. Minoru and company were able to rescue her before she sustained any physical harm, but the psychological shock at seeing Biter transformed up close had a large effect on her, and given that there was also a chance that she might be attacked again, she had been kept safe at a hospital connected with Chief Himi.

Tomomi, who after four days of hospitalization was able to calm down, had her memories associated with Biter sealed away by Chief Himi's power and supposedly returned to school Wednesday the week before. According to Oguu, even on the first day back, she also returned to practice for the track club that same day.

"Well... That's good to hear," said Minoru, lowering his shoulders along with his anxiety and took a bite of his Inari sushi.

However, Oguu's expression was still clouded. Staring at a tomato on his plate, he continued in a low voice. "She does seem fine...but I don't know. She seems a bit different from before she got hurt."

"..." Minoru paused.

There was no way they could let the truth out about the attack, so officially, Tomomi had been "injured while practicing on her own." Oguu, and possibly Tomomi herself, believed that that's what happened.

While Minoru felt bad about having to hide the truth from Oguu, who seemed genuinely concerned about Tomomi, he asked, "Different how? Has her running form changed or something?"

"No, it's nothing like that. Her times haven't gotten any slower, either; it's just when she's running...sometimes she has this really painful look on her face. No, *painful* might not be the right word to describe it... Ugh, I don't know how to put it exactly...," said Oguu, moaning a bit at the end, before popping the tomato into his mouth.

Maybe he didn't like tomatoes, because he grimaced as he ate it before washing it down with barley tea and looking at Minoru. Oguu scratched his head of shortly cut hair and then said in a rough manner, "...I know I don't have any right to be asking you something like this... I mean, I had my upperclassmen come to beat you up because I didn't like to see you and Minowa getting along... That was pretty damn uncool of me. I apologize for that. Seriously."

Oguu bowed his head so low it looked like he was about to stick his nose into the chicken on his plate and ignored the curious stares coming from the students around them. After holding that position for a little while, he lifted his head and with a serious look on his face said, "Utsugi, could you talk to Minowa for me?"

What do I say to that? was the phrase that ran through Minoru's head several times throughout his afternoon classes.

Minoru knew that he couldn't ignore Oguu's request, as Oguu was seriously worried about Tomomi Minowa, but ever since Tomomi had been discharged from the hospital, Minoru had been intentionally avoiding her.

There were two reasons for this. One was that if they talked, there was a chance that he might revive Tomomi's memories of Biter that Chief Himi had sealed away. The second reason was because he felt incredibly guilty in a way he couldn't even put into words.

Right before Tomomi had had her memories sealed away, Minoru had made a promise with her. The promise was, "If we meet again on the banks of the Arakawa River, we'll become friends again."

Minoru intended to honor that promise. But at the same time, he realized that he was being deceptive. After all, he had made a deal with Chief Himi that in exchange for joining the SFD, once all of the Ruby Eyes were exterminated, he would have everyone's memories of himself, including Tomomi's, erased.

Minoru didn't know if that would ever actually come to pass. Fear might drive him to leave the SFD, or he might be killed in a battle with the Ruby Eyes or sustain irreversible injuries just like Yumiko Azu's partner, Sanae Ikoma.

At the very least, Minoru's deal with Chief Himi contradicted his promise with Tomomi. From this point on, Minoru was going to fight as a Jet Eye in order to have the memories of himself erased from Tomomi.

Minoru had been worrying about this for the past few days, and as a result, he half looked forward to and half feared meeting Tomomi again on the banks of the Arakawa River in the morning and ended up avoiding her at school.

But really, what do I say to a request like that...? Minoru thought, sighing for what seemed like the hundredth time, just as the bell marking the end of sixth period rang.

Minoru got his things together and left the classroom, walking down the stairs. He changed into his shoes at his shoe locker, walked out of the front entrance, and then stood in place, looking left and right. If he was going to head to the bike parking lot, he needed to turn left, and if he was going to make his way to the school grounds area, he needed to turn right.

After a few moments of hesitation, Minoru turned right.

Minoru made his way to the grounds after a few minutes of walking and saw that the track club members were already doing warm-ups. The female members all had on light lavender tracksuits and were doing stretches. Minoru spotted the one with short hair he recognized and stared at her from across the fence.

He was probably fifty meters away, but perhaps because his eyesight had been improved by his Third Eye, Minoru was clearly able to see Tomomi's face. The reason she had a grimace on her face was probably because she was stretching her calves and Achilles tendons to their limit, Minoru thought. But just from her serious expression, Minoru wasn't able to read what was going on inside of her.

Well, if they've already started practice, it's not like I can call out to her or anything. No, even if they hadn't started, I couldn't do something that would leave a memory of me in all of the track club members... The watch on my left wrist says it's 3:50 p.m. The track club's practice should continue until around 7:00 p.m. Just standing around at the corner of the grounds would be too suspicious, so I should probably retreat to the library and then come back later, Minoru thought and turned to head back toward the main school building.

Minoru left the grounds and took a left turn past the gym. After walking a little bit after that, Minoru noticed footsteps approaching him from behind. By the time he had noticed them, they were already close by and slowing down.

It can't be, Minoru thought as he turned around, but next

to him jogging in place was Tomomi Minowa, who had been practicing with the track club not a minute before.

Tomomi, still jogging in place, looked up at Minoru, who froze from this unexpected development, and asked in a small voice, "...You were looking at me from the grounds just a second ago...weren't you?"

Apparently Tomomi also had exceptional eyesight. Minoru wasn't sure if Tomomi had identified him as "Minoru Utsugi from Class One," but he had no choice but to nod in response.

"Y-yeah..."

"...Why were you looking at me?"

Minoru had trouble answering this second sudden question and averted his gaze from Tomomi and looked down, thinking hard about what he would say.

Tomomi Minowa had had all of her memories related to Biter sealed away by Chief Himi. The problem was exactly what memories were included in that scope.

Tomomi should have forgotten that she'd been locked in that shed in Akigase Park, as well as the fact that Minoru had saved her. She probably also had forgotten about how she met Minoru in the park before that incident. However, it seemed that from how she was questioning him now, she might remember part of when she met Minoru in the morning on the banks of the Arakawa River two weeks ago.

That was probably not intentional on Chief Himi's part. Then, perhaps, if Minoru said something careless now, the seal on her memories might weaken, and there was a possibility that it might cause a chain reaction that would lead to her remembering everything about being attacked by Biter.

Minoru thought that he might avert the conversation by saying that he was thinking of joining the track club, but that was very unnatural given that it had been nine months since the start of the school year, and furthermore, he didn't want to lie. Minoru didn't think he had any other option but to tell the truth.

"Well... I actually wanted to talk about something... But since your club practice started, I thought I might wait for it to be over...," he said.

"You wanted to talk...to me?"

"...Yeah."

After Minoru nodded in response to Tomomi's third question, Tomomi stopped jogging in place and adjusted her stance. Her clean-cut hairstyle and large brown eyes were just as Minoru remembered, but he felt that compared to before, her brilliant, energetic nature was more muted and replaced with a certain melancholic, hesitant shadow that came over her expression.

Tomomi looked straight into Minoru's eyes and asked her fourth question in almost a whisper. "We've...talked before, haven't we?"

"...!" Not knowing how to respond, Minoru felt sweat form on his forehead, but Tomomi, who continued to stare at Minoru, suddenly let out a chuckle for some reason.

"Let's talk somewhere else. I'm going to go do road training right now, so could you follow me from a little distance behind me?" Tomomi said.

Minoru followed Tomomi, who was jogging very slowly, from about thirty meters behind about as fast as he could walk, as she led him to a small stream about two hundred meters east of the school.

When Tomomi stopped as she got to the road that ran along the stream, Minoru caught up to her about thirty seconds later. He stood next to her as she looked at the water's surface beyond a white chain-link fence.

Just as Minoru was wondering what to do, Tomomi asked, "...Do you know the name of this river?"

"...No, I don't," replied Minoru, blinking in response to that unexpected question, but Tomomi quickly gave the answer.

"Its name is the West Minuma Irrigation Canal."

"That's interesting..."

Minoru had learned about the Minuma Irrigation Canal in elementary school as part of his social studies class. A person named Sobee Izawaya constructed the canal, during the Edo period under the reign of Emperor Kyouhou in the early 1700s, as part of the Nitta Development Project under the orders of the eighth shogun Tokugawa Yoshimune. Minoru had a memory of riding a bus far upstream to look at the dams along it, but he had no idea it flowed this close to his high school.

"...Do you like rivers, Minowa?" Minoru asked as he looked down at the water's flow, and Tomomi responded with a short nod.

"I do. I think it's strange...that all this water keeps flowing without stopping even a single second. Far to the south, this stream flows into the Sasame River, and then the Sasame River flows into the Arakawa River," she said.

"Huh."

"Every morning, I run along the banks of the Arakawa River. It's calming to run while sensing the river's feelings, and it helps me concentrate..."

Minoru felt like he understood what she was talking about and nodded. "I think I understand what you mean. I also run along the banks of the Arakawa River every morning." But after he said that he realized he had made a mistake.

Feeling Tomomi's stare on his left cheek, Minoru slowly turned to look at her. When he did, he felt as though he had been pierced through by her eyes filled with a serious light and was unable to look away.

"You know, last week I was absent for a few days because of a light injury, but...something feels strange about it," she said.

"Strange?" Minoru replied.

"Past Hanekura Bridge, just a little farther upstream there's a barrier for traffic...and whenever I go past there, I find my feet stopping and my chest tightens. I feel as if something very frightening happened there...but also something that made me happy...," Tomomi continued.

"...Something frightening?" Minoru repeated, as his thoughts began to race desperately.

The car barrier near Hanekura Bridge... That was where, in the early morning on December 3, Minoru first ran into Tomomi. Tomomi seemed to have forgotten what happened, but as they were talking, a bike had come along at an incredible speed, and Minoru had protected her as it almost clipped her.

That certainly was a chilling experience, but at the same time he didn't think anyone would call it "very frightening." Maybe Tomomi was conflating that incident with the fear she felt when she was attacked by Biter in the adjacent Akigase Park. As Minoru looked at her, Tomomi closed her eyes tightly, furrowed her brow, and bit her lip as if she was trying to remember something. This had to be the "painful expression" that Oguu was talking about at lunch.

What should I do? Minoru thought. *Should I contact Chief Himi and have him reseal her memories? But would that help the situation at all? Tomomi would still continue to run along the banks of the Arakawa River, so the same thing might happen whenever she ran past the barrier...*

"...You're Utsugi, aren't you? We were in the same class in middle school," Tomomi said after slowly opening her eyes and staring at Minoru.

"...Yeah."

"Just a little while ago, you said you came to the grounds

because you said you wanted to talk to me about something, right? What is it?" Tomomi asked.

"Well..." He could tell her that it wasn't anything important. That he was sorry, that she shouldn't worry about it. Then, he could leave and never talk to her again. All things considered, that was his best option.

If the seal on her memories of meeting Minoru was unstable, he shouldn't do anything to make it worse. Even if that meant ignoring Oguu's request... Even if that meant breaking his promise to Tomomi about becoming friends again.

Even though that was what he thought intellectually, Minoru's mouth would not move. Somewhere deep in his chest he felt a sort of helplessness rising up and catching in his throat.

Three months ago, in an area with Tokyo at its center, mysterious spheres fell to Earth and infected dozens of people. Minoru was one of them, and so was Hikaru Takaesu, code name Biter.

As a result, Minoru was dragged into an extremely abnormal fate, but he had no intention of bemoaning his circumstances. After all, in a way, Minoru might have called this black sphere in his chest to himself.

However, Tomomi Minowa was not liable for these circumstances. Attacked by Biter, she was almost killed, and to top it all off she had her memories altered... There was no reason for her to have to feel these lingering feelings of fear, even after she returned to school.

"I made a promise with you," Minoru said, after a time. Tomomi's eyes opened wide.

"...A promise? What kind of promise...?" she asked.

"I promised that if I met you again, I would become friends with you," Minoru replied.

Since Tomomi shouldn't have any memory of that promise, Minoru had prepared for Tomomi to either laugh at him or think that he was being creepy, but he answered truthfully anyway. However, Tomomi had a serious look on her face and walked a half step closer to Minoru.

"...Are you talking about a promise made when we were in middle school? I'm sorry... I can't remember...," she said, twisting her face and pressing a finger from her left hand against her forehead as she tried to recall her memories. She seemed to be dizzy. Her small body started to tilt, and she hit her right shoulder against the white fence.

"Minowa, are you all right?!" Minoru quickly reached out his right hand to support her shoulder. Over her clothes he could feel that her small body was very cold, and again he felt as if something was caught in his throat.

Was it even right for Tomomi, suffering the shock of being attacked by such a monster as Biter, to have been treated only by the manipulation of her memories? Rather than forcefully putting a lid on that shock, wouldn't it have been better to carefully explain the situation and give her proper counseling? Was the reason Chief Himi sealed away her memories really for Tomomi's sake? Or was it just to protect the secret of the Third Eyes? Were they prioritizing the SFD or perhaps even a higher authority over Tomomi?

The moment Minoru thought that, he felt a strong anger well up inside him and he clenched his teeth. However, that emotion quickly turned to one of surprise. Tomomi had clasped both of her hands around Minoru's right hand and was holding it against her chest.

"Your hand is really warm...Utsugi," she said.

It's not as if Minoru could say that it was because of his Third Eye.

"...Well, it's because I'm wearing a lot of layers...," he said in a small lie.

Tomomi chuckled a little and looked up at him. "I'm sorry. I can't seem to remember making that promise with you... But if you're okay with that, I don't mind being friends," she said.

"Ah... O-of course! I mean, I'm sorry for bringing this up all of a sudden. It's no wonder you forgot about it. It was a really... really long time ago," Minoru replied.

"Well, okay... But it's kind of strange. This doesn't feel like the first time we've done this. When I'm with you like this, it feels like the fog in my head is starting to clear...," Tomomi said, closing her eyes with Minoru's hand still held against her chest.

The dry December north wind rushed past them and created ripples on the surface of the irrigation stream. Minoru instinctively moved to shield Tomomi, who seemed to shiver in the cold from the wind, taking her hand and pulling her closer. However, before he could do that, his smartphone vibrated in his coat pocket. Tomomi, who seemed to hear the noise and come to her senses, let go of Minoru's hand and took one step back.

"Um... Ha-ha, I'm sorry for being weird like that," she said, blushing, before starting to jog in place while slowly taking a few steps back. "But I'm really happy you asked me to be friends. Let's meet up some time and run along the banks of the Arakawa River!"

After saying that, Tomomi turned around and started running down the road along the irrigation stream at a fast pace. As Minoru watched her run away in her lavender tracksuit, he wondered to himself whether this really was for the best. But he knew that the answer to that question would only come after all of the incidents relating to the Third Eyes came to a close. For the time being, he could only do what he was able to do—even if once he got home, he ended up regretting the choice he'd made here.

After taking a deep breath in the cold air, Minoru took his smartphone out of his pocket. Displayed on the screen was a short text message that had arrived about ten seconds ago. The sender was Yumiko Azu, and the text was a single line:

"I'll be there to pick you up in ten seconds."

...*In ten seconds? In ten seconds from when?* Minoru thought, staring dumbfounded at the screen when immediately behind him—*vroom!*—he heard the loud but smooth rumble of an engine.

What Minoru saw as he nearly leaped, turning around, was a sport bike–type motorcycle with a pitch-black fairing, its rider dressed in a full-body black leather riding suit. Behind the rider's full-face helmet flowed long, straight black hair.

After setting the kickstand, the rider flipped a slender leg over the back of the bike and dismounted before lifting the visor on her helmet. As soon as Minoru saw the shining eyes within, he gave a shout.

"Y-Yumiko?!"

"Sorry for interrupting you in a good moment," Yumiko replied.

Her voice was a little bit muffled by the helmet, but there was no mistaking that it was her voice.

"It wasn't anything like that, but...why are you dressed like that?!" he asked.

"Well, I came here on a motorcycle, so this is pretty normal wear, right?" she replied.

"Ah, right... No, that's not what I mean!" said Minoru, flustered.

Ignoring Minoru, Yumiko set down her large backpack and took out a white roundish thing. Minoru, who reflexively took the object as Yumiko thrust it in front of him, realized it was the same kind of helmet Yumiko wore but a different color.

"...Umm...?"

"Put it on," said Yumiko.

"But I mean..."

As Minoru thought to himself that he had never worn one of these things and didn't know what to do, flipping it over in his hands, Yumiko grabbed the straps hanging from the helmet with both of her hands and forcefully put it on over his head. Just as Minoru was panicking from the sudden change, he heard Yumiko's voice incredibly clearly in his ear.

"Not bad. I think it suits you," she said.

From the nature of the sound, Minoru realized that there must be a speaker on the inside of the helmet, which also meant that there was probably a microphone as well.

"Umm… It's a little tight…"

"It used to be Sanae's. Later we'll have the inside padding switched out so that it fits you better, but you're going to have to bear with it today," Yumiko said, returning to the motorcycle and putting her empty backpack in the trunk compartment attached to the back of the motorcycle.

"Let me see your bag," Yumiko said, extending her right hand. Minoru gave her his school messenger bag, and once she put it away in the trunk compartment, she leaped back on the motorcycle.

"Get on behind me," she said.

Ever since he had the helmet put on his head, Minoru had figured that this was what was going to happen next, but he still took a hesitant step back.

"B-but I've never ridden a motorcycle before…"

"I'm not asking you to drive it or anything, all you have to do is hang on."

"…Okay," said Minoru, realizing that it was impossible for him to escape. After securely buttoning up his Chesterfield coat, he reluctantly mounted the rear seat. Since there was really no place to hang onto, he felt very anxious.

"Put both of your feet on the passenger foot pegs and hold onto my hips firmly with your knees," Yumiko said.

"Your…hips?" repeated Minoru before doing as Yumiko said and hesitantly gripping her slender hips between his knees.

"Good. Now position both hands around where my eighth ribs are and hold onto me," she continued.

"...Eighth?" repeated Minoru. It wasn't like he could touch and count her ribs from the top, so he guessed and wrapped his arms around her.

"Around here?" he asked.

"That's right. Now make sure you do not move your hands either up or down!" she commanded.

"O-okay."

"All right, let's go," Yumiko said, kicking back the kickstand and putting the motorcycle into gear.

The engine made a light rumble, and Yumiko deftly maneuvered the definitely-not-small motorcycle into a U-turn on the thin road beside the stream. Perhaps because she was paying mind to Minoru, a complete beginner, Yumiko drove slowly, and after a while they stopped at the light of an intersection right under the highway. Then, a group of elementary school boys, on their way from school, who were just crossing the crosswalk, all raised their voices at once and ran over.

"Whoa! That's so cool!"

"Hey, Miss, what kind of motorcycle is this?!"

Minoru thought that Yumiko would ignore them, but she gave a serious answer.

"It's an MV Agusta F3 800," she said.

"How much horsepower does it have?!"

"One hundred forty-eight horsepower," she replied.

"What's its top speed?!"

"Mach 0.7," she replied.

"No way!" all of the kids shouted at once.

It was at that moment that the light turned green, and after waving to the kids, Yumiko slowly set the motorcycle in motion.

After Yumiko took a right turn under the highway bridge and started speeding off down the lane, Minoru felt his shoulders drop as he relaxed and said, "So even you make jokes sometimes, huh?"

"What do you mean?"

"What? I mean with the kids just a second ago…," responded Minoru.

"I was being completely serious when I answered them. Also, isn't there something else that you should have asked me already?" asked Yumiko.

"Huh? …Oh, you mean that," said Minoru—perhaps because his feelings had finally caught up with the current state of things, a doubt he had left in the back of his mind resurfaced.

"Um… Why did you come to pick me up?" he asked.

"Igniter has made a move," Yumiko replied.

"What?!"

"Right now, DD and Oli-V are trailing him in a car. We're supposed to head him off."

Minoru felt his hands that were wrapped around Yumiko go sweaty, and he asked in a hoarse voice, "Does that mean we're…heading into battle?"

"Yes," Yumiko replied immediately with force in her voice, and Minoru flashed back to that room at SFD Headquarters where Sanae Ikoma lay sleeping.

"…Understood," Minoru replied. But getting just that one word out of his mouth took an enormous amount of effort.

Of course, this was not the first time Minoru would be fighting a red Third Eye host, also known as a Ruby Eye. Minoru had fought twice against Biter, who had attacked Tomomi Minowa and kidnapped his adoptive sister, Norie. However, both of those incidents were when he was passively caught up in a battle.

This time, though, as a member of the SFD, a black Third Eye host, and a Jet Eye, he was going to proactively attack a Ruby Eye and disable him. That is what Minoru now was going to do of his own volition. He was going to fight in a real life-and-death battle, with someone whose face and real name he did not know.

Just then, as if in an effort to cut off Minoru's cowardice, Yumiko flipped the turn signal on the large motorcycle. She drove the motorcycle through the entrance to the expressway headed for Tokyo, through the underground ETC gate, accelerating to eighty kilometers an hour through the tunnel.

I suppose, given that we are technically an organization under the Ministry of Health, Labor, and Welfare, Yumiko really does carefully obey the speed limit, huh, Minoru thought, even as his heart was racing given that this was the first time he had ever ridden at such speeds on a big sport bike.

But suddenly after, from above the trunk compartment on the back of the bike, right behind Minoru, rang a high-pitched siren sound. As Minoru jerked his head behind himself, he saw red flashing lights on both sides of the trunk compartment case.

"Wh-what is that?!" yelled Minoru.

"It's a siren and red emergency lights," Yumiko replied.

"D-did you just stick one on the motorcycle?" asked Minoru.

"Of course not. This is a proper siren obtained with the permission of the Public Safety Committee, according to Article 13 of the Enforcement Ordinance of the Road Traffic Act."

"And what do you plan on doing with this?!" Minoru yelled back.

"What do you think? This is dangerous, so make sure you hold on tight," she shot back, unperturbed, as she twisted the throttle in her right hand.

The engine gave a roar and the big bike shot forward into the passing lane as if it had been kicked. From over Yumiko's shoulder, Minoru could see the digital speedometer leap above one hundred kilometers an hour, closing in on 120.

After clearing a gentle left curve in the tunnel with a deep tilt of the motorcycle, they raced up an incline and onto a highway bridge. After another left following the road, they came upon a long straightaway on the Omiya section of the Tokyo-Saitama Expressway.

"It looks nice and clear, doesn't it?" said Yumiko, and just like she said, there were very few cars on the weekday evening section of the expressway headed for Tokyo.

Spurred on by a bad feeling about what was about to happen next, Minoru shouted, "I mean, since we're two people riding together, I think we should drive safely...!"

"Of course," replied Yumiko. "But we need to get to Ikebukuro in five minutes."

"What?! Five minutes?! There's no way!!" shouted Minoru.

The distance from Saitama's new urban center to Ikebukuro was more than twenty kilometers by road. Even if a person traveled at an average of one hundred kilometers an hour, it would take at least twelve minutes. If they wanted to reach Ikebukuro in five minutes, they would have to speed at 240 kilometers an hour. Even if they were treated as an emergency vehicle, there was no way they could go that speed on a public road and Minoru didn't think that it was even physically possible.

But Yumiko had apparently sensed Minoru's thoughts, and he heard her voice again over the intercom. "Igniter last used his power thirty-seven minutes ago in Shinjuku. Even with DD's power, there's only about five more minutes he can track him based on his lingering scent. So we've only got five minutes. So I'm going to send us flying. Hold on tighter."

"R-roger...," said Minoru, who took a deep breath and held on as tightly as he could around Yumiko's hips with his knees and around her waist with his arms. Only three seconds later did he learn the true meaning of what Yumiko meant when she said "send us flying."

Yumiko dropped the motorcycle, which was cruising at 120 kilometers an hour, two gears and twisted the accelerator with her right hand all the way. The engine roared as the rotations per minute of the engine leaped up. As the front wheel rose slightly above the ground, the steel frame of the large motorcycle shot forward like a bullet.

Acceleration.

That was Yumiko's power. Yumiko, who was given the code name Accelerator, amplified her own acceleration to charge forward almost instantaneously. If the bike's engine power fell within the scope of "her own acceleration"...

"You've got to be kidding me...," muttered Minoru as an unnatural and overwhelming force sent the motorcycle flying forward a few centimeters above the ground at an incredible speed.

The highway and sunset-filled sky melted into a radial blur around them. The air pressure came at them like a wall, and Minoru clung desperately to Yumiko's body. If Minoru didn't have the strength of a Jet Eye, he might have been thrown from the bike and tumbled onto the road.

Minoru stared dazed as a large truck in the distance looked as small as a grain of rice, then came flying at them, as if he were watching a video sped up to twenty times its normal speed.

By the time Minoru was able to scream, the motorcycle's front wheel had come down, screeching as it contacted the road and retained its grip. The truck was right before their eyes in an instant.

Reducing the speed to 120 kilometers an hour, Yumiko lightly tilted the motorcycle and passed the truck on the left.

When they were all clear again, as Yumiko stared down the road, she said, "I said earlier, didn't I? That this motorcycle's top speed is Mach 0.7." Then, before Minoru could say anything, she opened the throttle again.

Unable to do anything else, Minoru let out another loud scream.

9

Making himself comfortable in the backseat of a taxi, Ayato Suka slowly exhaled. It was long ago that smoking had been banned in taxis throughout the Tokyo metropolitan area, but the inside of the vehicle gave off the odor of new smoke. Trying not to click his tongue, Suka opened the left passenger window all the way.

Sending the unpleasant smell of the car heater along with the odor of the smoke out the window, Suka instead took a deep breath of the sharp, cold outside air. Of course, the outside air was full of the exhaust from all of the cars passing by on Meiji Street, but it was at least better than the unbearable air inside the taxi.

"Excuse me, sir. I do have the heater on, you know?" complained the forty-something-year-old taxi driver, but Suka quickly replied.

"Then turn it off, it's too hot in here," he said, ignoring the taxi driver as he loudly clicked his tongue, and once again Suka took a deep breath—this time through his nose—and paid close attention to the scent.

Mixed in with the exhaust very faintly was that one particular odor. It was a kind of chemical smell that prickled the scent-sensing cells of his nose.

It was *their* scent. The scent of the black hunters.

Both the "reds," like Suka, and the "blacks," their enemies, could sniff out each other's existence. Fundamentally that scent could only be detected when they were using their powers, but Suka's sense of smell was a bit of a special case. Perhaps it was a beneficial side effect of being able to manipulate oxygen over a wide area, but he could detect when he was being chased by the enemy. However, the range of that detection was only two kilometers. In other words, right now, they were closing in on him.

"Keep going on Meiji Street and then take a right on Kasuga Street," said Suka to the taxi driver, as he leaned back into the seat.

Even though Suka knew the danger of being chased, at the same time he felt a deep satisfaction rising from the pit of his stomach. Again today, he burned a fool who did not understand the preciousness of oxygen and sacrificed him for the sign he planned to draw in the city center. Furthermore, the time it took him to carbonize the body so that no bones were left behind was nearly a minute less than before. He really wanted to burn a second person, but he thought he should be satisfied with his results for the day.

His power to manipulate oxygen was still improving. At this rate, the day he reached a new stage of his power was not far in the future. When that time came, in the pure shine of combustion, he would oxidize all of those annoying black hunters together.

I am different from Liquidizer and the rest of her organization, those who have thrown away their righteous calling just to concentrate on staying alive, Suka thought.

Suka's calling was to take back the oxygen cycle on this planet. In that cycle, there was no place for the filthy combustion done by humans.

"Ha-ha." As Suka held back the desire to hum his oxygen song, he instead let out a short chuckle from deep inside his throat. The taxi driver gave him an unnerved look through the rearview mirror, but Suka didn't care.

* * *

Just as Yumiko had declared, they went a distance of twenty kilometers in just under five minutes. There were often times that its wheels were off the ground, but the large motorcycle finally turned off the expressway at the East Ikebukuro Interchange.

As soon as the siren and beacon on the back of the motorcycle stopped, Minoru leaned forward against Yumiko, exhausted. But immediately after he did so, he heard her voice over the intercom.

"It's way too early for you to be tired," she said. "Soon we'll have caught up to Igniter. You have the air tank that Professor gave you with you, right?"

"Y-yes…," replied Minoru.

"Then get it ready while we still have time," Yumiko said.

But just then Minoru remembered. He did have the compressed air tank with him, but while he was at school he didn't have it in his pocket, but in his…

"Ah… I'm sorry, it's in my bag in the back…," he said.

"…All right. I'll make a quick stop somewhere, so hurry up and…," Yumiko started, but just then another voice Minoru recognized came in over the intercom.

"This is Searcher. Accelerator, where are you right now?" There was a lot of noise on the channel, but there was no mistaking that it was DD.

Yumiko answered quickly, "East Ikebukuro, right under Sunshine."

"We're heading north on Meiji Street right now, but we're losing the scent. Igniter should be right on top of you. Do whatever you can to find him somehow!"

"Somehow… Just how many cars do you think I can see right now?" Yumiko replied.

"Just do whatever you can!! We'll meet up with you shortly. End of transmission!"

Just then, Yumiko's back, with Minoru still attached to her, sank dejectedly.

"He says things like they're so easy… Uts— I mean, Isolator, that's the situation right now, so look around at all of the cars, and if something pops out at you, tell me!" she said.

What am I even supposed to be looking for? Minoru thought, but he scanned what he could see, left and right.

Given that the one photograph of Igniter he was shown at SFD Headquarters was unclear and shot from a long distance away, all he knew was that he was a thin man. Plus, most of the people driving by in cars fit that description.

"Everyone kind of looks suspicious... Yu— I mean, Miss Accelerator, you've seen Igniter directly, right?" asked Minoru.

"Drop the 'Miss.' The one time I did see him was for a split second, and he was wearing a knit cap, sunglasses, and a mask."

"I see... Thanks. That'll come in handy," said Minoru, expanding the scope of his search.

Just above Minoru was the No. 5 Ikebukuro line Expressway bridge, from which they had just exited the expressway. The giant building with brick tiles to the right was probably Sunshine City. To the left, across a walkway, ran rows of fashionable shops, and all around were countless cars.

"...For the time being, I'll turn at the intersection and make a stop up ahead, so when I do, prepare your air tank," said Yumiko.

"All right," replied Minoru, just as his eyes reflexively settled on a single taxi.

＊ ＊ ＊

I don't believe it, thought Suka, aghast, as he stared at the taxi driver.

Even though he was in the middle of driving a customer, he had taken up a pack of cigarettes and pulled one out with his mouth. Tossing the pack to the side, he then took out a lighter and lit up without a second thought. After breathing out a large puff of smoke, as if he were shoving it in Suka's face, only then did he open up the driver's window.

When their eyes met in the mirror, after letting out a long, thin stream of smoke from his mouth, the driver smirked. "Ah, sorry about that. This is a personal taxi, so we're free to smoke. Feel free to take a smoke yourself."

The Tokyo Society of Personal Taxis banned smoking eleven years ago in 2008. Even disregarding that, what was he thinking smoking while he had a passenger? Was he really so childish that this was his way of getting back at Suka for not closing the window?

Suka was on the verge of saying, "I'm getting off. Stop the car now," but he swallowed his words at the last moment.

His shock and disbelief coupled with oxygen in the core of his brain, which quickly turned to murderous intent.

I'll burn him. I'll turn that head of his along with his cigarette to ash, he thought, but just as he raised his right hand, his reason slammed on the brakes.

Now was not the time. He was being chased. Using his power right now was like calling out to the black hunters and asking them to find him.

But still..., he thought, unable to bear it.

The oxygen in the car was being eaten away by a filthy form of combustion. The carbon dioxide and harmful substances entered his lungs with every breath, polluting his blood.

Even if he were to resist burning the driver and just exited the car, he would be tracked down by the black hunters before he found another taxi.

...I have no other choice, he thought and pulled something out of his favorite bag that he always had prepared for just such an occasion. It was an oxygen canister, the kind that could be picked up at any sports department store.

With a clear mask, he covered his nose and mouth and

pressed the button on the small canister. With the small sound of rushing air, a sweet, thick gas came flowing out. As he closed the window with a small grin, the taxi driver opened his eyes wide.

* * *

...What was that? thought Minoru as something crossed his line of sight and drew his attention.

It was a white taxi, and the driver was—outrageously in this day and age—smoking inside the car. But that was not what caught Minoru's attention. The passenger in the backseat of the taxi had something strange held to his mouth.

"...I'm sorry, could you make a U-turn?" said Minoru to Yumiko over the intercom.

"Did you find him?!" shouted Yumiko.

"N-no, I can't be sure yet, but something caught my eye...," started Minoru.

"What did you see?!" shouted Yumiko again.

Even as she was throwing questions at Minoru, she quickly put her turn signal on and made a turn into the oncoming lane, as soon as it was clear. The taxi was about ten cars ahead.

"Do you think you can catch up with that white taxi?" asked Minoru.

"Of course."

Yumiko opened the throttle in the left lane and accelerated between the right lane and the stopped cars on the left. They were getting closer and closer to the taxi.

As they pulled up alongside the taxi, Minoru looked into the passenger's seat through the window. The passenger still had something placed against his mouth. It was an O_2 can, the kind that one might use when climbing a mountain.

In other words, it was oxygen.

Gulping, Minoru stared at the man's face. But then his

shoulders relaxed and he whispered into the intercom, "I'm sorry, this isn't him."

It couldn't be. After all, the passenger, a man in a suit, was an elderly man who couldn't possibly be less than sixty. His half-white hair was carefully combed back, and his dry skin had deep wrinkles. He had an intellectual air about him that made him look like a teacher and not at all like a serial murderer. He probably had some disease that made it necessary to use an oxygen canister to breathe.

If you could make another U-turn, Minoru started to say to Yumiko but stopped. "Um… I'm going to activate my shell for a second."

"What?! Why?!"

"I think I'm wrong, but I just want to make sure," he said, unwrapping his arms from around Yumiko's body and taking a deep breath.

Minoru then held his breath and "pushed" against the pitch-black sphere in the middle of his chest.

"What do you mean by 'wr—' " Yumiko's voice was suddenly cut off.

The sound of the motorcycle engine, the sounds of the surrounding cars, and all of the other noise went silent. Minoru's vision took on a slight blue tint. His hips and legs levitated slightly above the motorcycle. With his three-centimeter-thick defensive shell, Minoru was isolated from the world.

Still, not much change could be seen from the outside. Even if the old man had been looking at Minoru, he probably wouldn't have realized that Minoru wasn't directly touching the seat of the motorcycle.

But…

A half second after Minoru activated his shell, the old man in the taxi leaped up and looked at Minoru from across the window. The sharp gaze Minoru felt from the man pierced both the window of the taxi and the faceplate of Minoru's helmet, straight into his eyes. Minoru stared on, surprised, as he saw the expression on the old man's face change from shock to that of a deep red intent to kill.

* * *

Suddenly, the inside of Suka's nostrils flamed up. There was a chemical smell so strong it felt as if it were going to burn away the scent-sensing cells of his nose.

For a second, Suka thought that the taxi driver had sprayed him with pepper spray, but in the next instant he realized, with a shiver, what that smell meant.

It was the scent of the black hunters. It was a signal that let him know that they had used their power. However, this was the first time he had ever felt so strong a scent. Even the time that that young girl had stabbed him in the stomach with a knife, the scent had not been this strong.

For some reason the smell quickly disappeared, but he turned his head to look left, as if he were being sucked in. Right outside the window was a black motorcycle running alongside the taxi. The driver, in a black leather jumpsuit, was looking straight ahead at the road, but a passenger riding behind was looking straight at him. Because of the helmet's faceplate, he could not see the passenger's face, but Suka was certain it was him.

It's that one. There's a black hunter just a meter away from me, using some power of his to capture his prey..., Suka thought.

A hatred he could not control welled up from his stomach, and Suka clenched his teeth together, bringing wrinkles to his nose.

Immediately afterward, Suka realized his mistake.

The one riding the motorcycle must have activated his power to test Suka's reaction. Feeling something strange about the fact that Suka was using an oxygen canister, he must have revealed his scent to test if Suka was really a red Third Eye host.

In other words, being surprised at the smell, looking left, and expressing his hatred had been a threefold mistake.

Suka's hatred mixed with humiliation and transformed into an overwhelming rage.

I'll kill him, no matter what it takes, Suka thought.

Transferring his oxygen canister to his left hand, Suka raised his right hand toward the motorcycle.

* * *

The moment Minoru saw the face of an old man who he guessed might be in his sixties, something in his memory tingled, but he didn't have the time to figure out why. The old man had raised his right hand, bending his five fingers into a claw. The middle of his palm split open horizontally to show a crimson sphere.

The sphere, which looked like a living eye, gave off a light the color of blood. Suppressing an instinctive desire to hide away in his shell, Minoru deactivated his power. Given that their prior conversation was cut off, it seemed that Minoru's shell cut off the wireless communication of the intercom as well. With his shell activated, he could not communicate with Yumiko.

The moment he sunk back into his seat on the motorcycle, he yelled in a hoarse voice, "Igniter is in the taxi to our right! We're going to be attacked!"

"…!!"

Minoru heard a sharp intake of air over the intercom. Immediately afterward, Minoru felt a rush of air from his right side, flowing left. It wasn't that strong of a wind, but it took away Minoru's breath. Flustered, Minoru tried to breathe in deeply, but the pain in his chest would not go away.

The air was thin.

This was Igniter's oxygen deprivation attack. It was likely that oxygen that Minoru and Yumiko should be breathing was being collected in a place away from the motorcycle. Minoru's lungs hurt as if they were being wrung out by something. The scene in front of Minoru's eyes grew dark. Minoru thought to breathe through the compressed air canister, but then realized that the canister he had been given by Professor Riri Isa was still in the motorcycle's trunk compartment.

I'll just reactivate my defensive shell, thought Minoru as he gasped for air. He didn't understand why, but he never lacked oxygen inside his shell. In other words, he should be able to defend against Igniter's oxygen deprivation attack.

But he couldn't do it. He couldn't breathe. In order to activate his protective barrier, he needed to fill his lungs with air and hold his breath. But right now, it felt as if something was caught in his throat, and no matter how he tried to breathe in, his lungs wouldn't respond.

...This...might be a problem, thought Minoru dizzily, as if he were thinking about someone else. Minoru's black Third Eye beat firmly against his ribs.

I wonder if it will eject itself, thought Minoru. Realizing that its host was about to die, maybe it would return to the sky, just like how the Third Eye leaped from Biter's corpse in the Saitama Super Arena underground parking lot.

At that moment...

"We're going to jump! Hold on!" came a voice screaming over the intercom, which brought Minoru back to his senses. With all of his remaining strength, he gripped onto Yumiko's body.

Perhaps due to the lack of oxygen, the motorcycle's engine had been whining, but it now suddenly roared a bestial roar.

An intense force traveled from the engine through the chain to the rear wheel and then to the street. Due to the counter torque, or a reactive moment of force in the opposite direction of the rear wheel, the front wheel rose in the air. Yumiko used her power to take that diagonally upward acceleration and amplify it.

Ka-boom!

With a crashing sound, the bike with its two riders leaped into the air at a ferocious speed, and the deep red evening sky spread out through Minoru's clouded vision.

* * *

They shouldn't have been able to escape, thought Suka.

He had moved the oxygen around the two black hunters a full ten meters away from them. Suka expected both the rider and passenger to immediately faint after they breathed in oxygen-deprived air.

Really, Suka wanted to aim for the motorcycle's engine. Inside the internal combustion engine, gasoline aerosol was constantly being burned. Even an elementary school student would be able to tell a person what would happen if he concentrated oxygen in that spot.

But unfortunately, the motorcycle was too close. If he caused the engine to explode, the taxi Suka was riding in would not escape unscathed. In the worst-case scenario, a scrap of the motorcycle could come flying through the glass window into the taxi. Therefore, as a second-best option, he had attacked by depriving them of oxygen, but...

"Wha...?!" said Suka in surprise, loosening the grip of his right hand.

The large motorcycle, which should have been caught in the oxygen-deprived area, suddenly pulled a flashy wheelie and then shot up diagonally into the air like an antiaircraft missile.

That was probably due to the power of the one who stabbed

him deep in the stomach, Suka thought. The driver wearing the black jumpsuit must have been her.

The frustration at letting his mortal enemy get away burned in the pit of his stomach, but that feeling only lasted an instant. It was not yet time to fight them. He had already prepared a proper stage for that battle somewhere else. It was important that he acted his age and moved forward with composure.

With the mask for his oxygen canister still pressed against his face with his left hand, Suka gave instructions to the taxi driver. "Stop the car at that intersection over there," he said.

However, the driver, still with a cigarette in his mouth, stretched his neck over the steering wheel and looked up at the sky from the front windshield.

"Did you see that, old man?! That motorcycle just flew into the air! Are they filming some sort of stunt?!"

It wouldn't have been unusual if the lack of oxygen in the surrounding air had affected the driver, but he had shut the window and seemed to have escaped the effect. Holding back his irritation, Suka repeated his instruction.

"I don't care. Stop the car," he said.

"All right, all right," replied the taxi driver, turning on his hazard lights and parking on the side of the road. As he was messing with the taximeter, he opened his mouth again. "Plus, didn't you give that motorcycle a signal or something a second ago, old man? Are you an actor or something?!" he said in a loud voice.

"..." Suka paused. *You really just said too much, didn't you, young one?* he thought.

Putting his oxygen canister back in his bag, Suka stretched out his right hand and gripped the taxi driver's oily neck from behind.

Snap.

By only applying a fraction of his strength, Suka had

pulverized the bones of the man's neck. To Suka's right hand, which he had strengthened and refined during his training in the mountains, human bone was nothing more than Styrofoam.

With only his right hand, Suka moved the slumped body of the driver into the passenger's seat and stepped out of the taxi. He went around to the driver's seat and got back in. After shoving the corpse down into the foot space of the passenger's seat, he set the taxi's sign to OUT OF SERVICE and started driving off.

* * *

As he struggled with the pain in his chest, Minoru was conscious of the fact that the motorcycle had leaped, no, soared, into the air.

Amplifying the acceleration of the motorcycle in a diagonally upward direction, Yumiko had caused it to lift off from the ground. It was an extreme use of her power, but at the same time it was probably the only way to have escaped the situation.

Even so, just how are we going to land? Minoru thought.

The motorcycle was coasting more than thirty meters up in the air. Obviously, there was no road beneath the wheels. They shouldn't be able to accelerate or decelerate any more.

However, Yumiko's body continued to support Minoru without flinching, even as Minoru was starting to lose consciousness.

Immediately afterward, the motorcycle reached its peak in flight and began to fall. If they ran into a building from this height, not only the bike, but also even as Third Eye hosts they were sure to take a massive amount of damage.

There was no way that Minoru alone could escape to the safety of his defensive shell, and even if he tried, he wasn't sure he could use his power as he was starting to lose consciousness.

In the direction of their fall, there were several low buildings with green-painted roofs. One of those they were approaching at a fast pace. Minoru thought that they were going to crash into that building in a matter of seconds, but his prediction turned out to be wrong.

The instant before they had reached the long rectangular building, the motorcycle immediately slowed its descent, as if it had deployed a parachute in midair.

They continued to approach the concrete rooftop, and both wheels landed at about the same time.

The deeply sinking suspension groaned as it absorbed the shock. Then, as the brakes were deployed, sparks leaped from the rotors as the motorcycle stopped in the center of the roof.

It seemed they'd escaped falling to their deaths, but why did their speed immediately drop in midair? Minoru wondered for a bit and then suddenly realized.

As the motorcycle fell, there was a drop in speed caused by air resistance, and a decrease in speed implies a negative acceleration, which naturally was the same in nature as a positive acceleration. Yumiko probably amplified that deceleration in order to brake the bike midair.

Accelerator...what an astounding power..., Minoru thought as he felt his consciousness quickly fall away from himself.

Minoru only hazily felt how he slipped from the rear seat of the motorcycle and tumbled onto the concrete roof.

"...!!" Yumiko screamed something Minoru could not quite hear, rushed over, and pulled up the lower half of his body. After yanking off his helmet, Yumiko pulled the small mouthpiece popping out from the neck of her jumpsuit and stuck it into Minoru's mouth.

"...the! Breathe!!" she shouted, and Minoru tried to follow her instructions, but his lungs no longer responded. It was as if hot glue had been washed down his windpipe and into his lungs, hardening over his entire respiratory system. Minoru's vision grew darker with every second, and he could feel his Third Eye throb deep within his chest.

Is this an...emotion? Is it...anger? Or...sadness?

The mouthpiece was suddenly taken out of his mouth.

Yumiko put it into hers and bent backward, breathing in deep. She then spit out the mouthpiece, and without a moment's hesitation, she locked lips with Minoru. After securing the airway and holding Minoru's nose, she vigorously exhaled. The oxygen-rich gas wrenched open his windpipe and flowed into his lungs.

Yumiko pulled her face back and put the mouthpiece in her mouth again. She took another deep breath of the high-oxygen-content-enriched air that Professor Riri had procured for them and transferred it again into Minoru's mouth.

Unable to think about anything at all, his body frantically devoured the oxygen that was given to him. As the burning pain in his lungs was washed away, the throbbing of his Third Eye that had felt as if it were going to explode quickly subsided.

"...hn...! Kugh...!!"

With a cough, Minoru's lungs finally began to work on their own.

Yumiko looked directly into Minoru eyes and shouted, "Can you breathe?! Can you breathe on your own now?!"

"Y... Ye-yes...," said Minoru in a raspy voice.

At that moment, Minoru felt something warm and wet dripping onto his cheek. It took a few moments for him to realize that it was Yumiko's tears. Yumiko seemed to be surprised by her own tears as well and pulled back. She wiped her eyes several times on the sleeve of her jumpsuit, but eventually she gave up, turning her back to Minoru and hunching over as her shoulders shook.

Minoru couldn't say anything, nor could he even get up, so he just continued to stare at her back.

Only the clicking sound of the cooling motorcycle overlapped with Yumiko's sobs.

10

As the old elevator opened noisily onto the fourth floor, Yumiko said, "I'm going to stop by my room," and walked out. The door then closed, and the elevator continued to ascend. It had been three days since Minoru visited SFD Headquarters, but the fifth floor welcomed Minoru as before with its wide expanse. There was still a lingering bit of red light from the sky that shone in through the windows on the south side. Minoru thought it strange that even on his second visit he had arrived at around the same time.

Minoru had left school at 3:55 p.m. He and Tomomi Minowa parted ways on the road by the irrigation stream at 4:20 p.m. Immediately afterward, he was picked up by Yumiko on her motorcycle, and they arrived at Ikebukuro at 4:30 p.m. They then approached Igniter, but due to Minoru's negligence let him get away, and Professor Riri gave the order to retreat to headquarters. Everything had happened in the course of an hour.

...Not to mention that I almost died from Igniter's oxygen-deprivation attack and was saved by Yumiko..., Minoru thought. Even after he stepped out of the elevator, he stood in front of the doors, mulling over that fact.

Yumiko was still on the fourth floor, and Minoru didn't see Riri or DD when he looked around the room.

Instead, in front of the large TV, sitting hunched over, was someone he had not seen before. From what he could see, it was a male and probably a high school student. He was wearing a blazer that had the same color scheme as Yumiko's. He had large headphones on his head and was holding a game controller in both hands.

Minoru ventured over, wondering if he should say something. The TV screen entered his view. On the screen was an early RPG-type video game for a system that had come out long before Minoru was even born. Because the resolution of the game was only a few hundred dots in either direction and it was displayed on a sixty-five-inch LCD screen, every pixel was ridiculously big.

Minoru watched on silently as the protagonist's party on the right attacked with simple pastoral animations. It reminded him of the handheld games he used to play together with his sister Wakaba before the incident. Even though those were of a far higher resolution, he thought that even the kind of game being played in front of him might be entertaining in its own way.

After the protagonist's party easily disposed of the monsters and the screen returned to the field, the game was paused.

The male high school student, who was sitting cross-legged on a cushion, leaned back onto the floor and looked up, with controller still in hand, upside down at Minoru. After a smirk, he lifted himself and sprang to his feet smoothly without using his hands and turned toward Minoru.

When they faced each other, the high school student was about three centimeters taller than Minoru. He had longish wavy brown hair, and below his bangs were blue plastic-framed glasses. The irises of his eyes behind his glasses were large and well proportioned, the bridge of his nose was high, and the outlines of his face were both sharp and stylish. No matter how you looked at him, he certainly didn't look very Japanese.

In part because of his unaffected smile, Minoru was just able to step forward and introduce himself.

"Um… It's nice to meet you. I'm Utsugi. I just joined the SFD a few days ago," Minoru said.

Whereupon the high school student stared at Minoru with his pale eyes and asked an unexpected question.

"Are you the kind of person who levels up your characters?

Or are you the kind who tries to get through the game on the lowest level possible?"

...*What?* Minoru thought, taken aback, but he answered truthfully. "I haven't played any games recently...but I tend to like to play for a long time, so I do a ton of leveling."

The student broke out into a friendly smile and extended his right hand. "I'm the kind who levels up so much that I kill the last boss instantaneously. ...The name's Olivier Saito. Looking forward to working with you."

...*O-Olivier?*

If that's his real name...did that mean he's half Japanese, half French?

No wonder he's so cool, thought Minoru, shaking Olivier's hand, flinching in his strong grip. He was definitely a Third Eye host.

After squeezing Minoru's right hand for a little while, Olivier Saito patted him on the shoulder and said, "All right! Let's get to work together doing some unnecessary leveling! I'm just about to level up, so after that, I'll let you join in."

Without waiting for Minoru to answer, Olivier sat back in front of the TV, controller in hand. Before Minoru could even break out of the pose he held from Olivier's introduction, he heard an incredulous voice behind him.

"Hey, Oli-V, don't go and make the newbie your level-up slave."

When Minoru turned around, right behind him was Denjirou "DD" Daimon, with his trademark cap put on backward.

"Hurry up and save your game, man. If you're still doing that when the time comes for our meeting, Yumiko'll pull the plug on you," he said.

"Yeah, I really don't want to repeat that tragedy," said Olivier, shrugging his shoulders, before saving the game and turning off both the cutting-edge TV and the old system connected to it.

"Sorry 'bout that, Utsugi. What was your code name again...? 'Isolator'? Anyway, we'll have to have fun leveling up some other time."

"Su-sure, absolutely," Minoru replied, surprised that Olivier knew about him.

Just a minute ago, DD had called Olivier "Oli-V," and Minoru had heard that nickname before. He was one of the SFD members who were out tracking Igniter when Minoru came to headquarters before.

...Which means that Olivier and DD are partners? Minoru thought to himself as he watched them walk ahead of him. Even though they looked mismatched, something about them both seemed to fit, and Minoru unthinkingly cast his eyes down.

Minoru had remembered that he made a huge mistake on his very first mission that he was partnered with Yumiko and wanted to run away somewhere.

But then, Minoru heard the sound of the elevator reaching the fifth floor. Riri Isa, who followed Yumiko out of the elevator, took one look at Minoru, DD, and Olivier and said, "I see you're all here! Well, then, let's start the meeting!"

While Minoru was listening to Yumiko, who had changed out of her leather jumpsuit and into her uniform, give her report, he spent the whole time making himself look small.

Professor Riri, who stood in front of the eighty-inch monitor, sighed once the report had reached a pause. "You let him get away, huh...? We were so close this time..." She then turned her gaze to DD.

"How far were you able to track him?"

As DD answered, he had a stern look on his face. "We found the taxi that Igniter was riding in at the small underpass at West Ogu in the Arakawa district. There was a corpse in the passenger seat of the car, but the cause of death was not burning or suffocation but due to a compound compression fracture of his cervical vertebrae. It is unclear where Igniter went after he left, and the drive recorder for the taxi was also removed."

"I see. Did screening for fingerprints and other forensic tests bring up any results?" Riri asked.

"I was not able to get any fingerprints off of the victim's neck," DD continued. "Instead, I found residue from liquid bandages, which he must be putting on his hands to hide his fingerprints. I found many fingerprints and hair follicles in the backseat, but to be honest, I don't see us pulling any useful information from all of that."

"You're probably right," Riri said. "Sifting through the countless passengers who rode in that taxi to find leads would be very difficult... I guess our last hope depends on Mikkun's memory."

His name suddenly called, Minoru shrank away even more.

"...Mikkun. You're the only one who has gotten a clear look at Igniter's face up close. Now this is an old-fashioned way of doing things, but I think it's worth a try," Riri continued, pulling a sketchbook, pencil, and eraser from a desk in front of the monitor.

Minoru, who had a bad feeling about what was going to happen next, asked, "...Umm, what is it exactly that you want me to do with that?"

"What do you think? I want you to draw Igniter's face," she replied.

Ten minutes later.

After a long and difficult battle with the sketchbook, Minoru handed it over to Professor Riri. The fact that Riri's expression didn't change one bit, even after she flipped the cover to look inside, was testament to a level of restraint well beyond her age.

"...Hmm," she said and then carefully tore out the page and took it to a nearby scanner, and it was immediately enlarged and displayed on the screen.

The first one to react was Olivier. He leaned back in his chair, barely keeping from flipping over, and kicked both of his legs in the air as he laughed. "Bwa-ha-ha-ha-ha-ha! You call that a human?! It looks like a hobgoblin or something to me!"

"Hey, Oli-V. Minoru gave it his best shot, so it's wrong to laugh...fwa-ha..." Even DD seemed to have trouble containing his laughter, and it sounded like he had a hard time breathing.

Minoru had expected this, but even he got a little hurt to be laughed at so much, so he retorted, "...I've never drawn anyone's face before, so... Anyway! Igniter is a thin man who looks like he's in about the first half of his sixties, with whitening hair all pulled back... The kind of person who you might think would be the vice-principal of a school."

After adding that explanation, Minoru returned to his seat and Riri clapped her hands twice together.

"Now, Oli-V, DD, stop laughing. This is valuable information. I'll put together a montage later based on this. He...is a lot older than I expected. Mikkun, is there anything else in particular that you remember about him?" asked Riri.

Minoru sat silent, thinking. As his gaze wandered, Olivier and DD were still shaking with laughter, but Yumiko's face was completely expressionless. On their way back to headquarters, after letting Igniter get away, Yumiko had hardly said a word.

When they got off the bike, Minoru had thanked her again for saving his life, but she had just nodded without meeting his eye. At first he had thought that she was embarrassed for crying in front of him, but he had a feeling that it was something else. It seemed as if she had shut herself away inside her own heart...

After shaking off those thoughts, Minoru replied to Riri,

"Well...now that you mention it, I felt as if I had seen him somewhere before."

"Really? Recently?" Riri asked.

"No...and I didn't think that when I saw the side of his face, but when he looked straight at me, I thought, *Huh?* for a second and got that feeling," he said.

The moment Igniter had turned to face Minoru when he activated his power, with that intent to kill in his eyes, Minoru had felt a very faint stimulation of his memories. However, Minoru was terrible at remembering faces. He couldn't even remember the face of the librarian he saw at the library nearly every day and at least once every three days, so it was unthinkable for him to remember the face of someone who, for instance, he had just passed by one day on the street.

"...I'm sorry. I can't remember," Minoru muttered, and Riri looked down, her expression melancholy.

"I see... Well, while I'm putting together the montage, you might remember something else. For now I'll call this meeting to a close. DD, I would like you to continue to be on the lookout for Igniter. Everyone else is to be on standby until we have any new information."

"Oh, before that, can I have a minute?"

"Hm? What is it, Oli-V?" asked Riri.

Olivier Saito, who seemed to finally get his convulsions of laughter under control, stood up in a graceful motion and turned his bluish-gray eyes toward Yumiko.

"Yumiko, in the report you gave earlier there was one part that I didn't quite understand. You said that you found Igniter, was attacked, and retreated, right? Why didn't you launch a counterattack?" Olivier asked.

With her head down, Yumiko visibly twitched.

Minoru also fidgeted in his chair. In her report, Yumiko had omitted part of what had happened.

In other words, she had omitted the fact that Minoru had inhaled oxygen-deprived air and had nearly died.

Yumiko went silent for a little while, but then finally said, "Because it was dangerous."

"Well, obviously. We're fighting Ruby Eyes, you know?" Olivier replied. His attitude was still easygoing, but there was a sharpness in the tone of his voice. "But I mean, if we keep running away instead of fighting, just because it's dangerous, is there really any meaning in us being here at all?"

"...Wait! Umm...," said Minoru, finding his determination and standing up. Minoru needed to explain that Yumiko was not at fault. Minoru looked steadily at Olivier's well-proportioned face and continued on, stuttering.

"Umm... It's my fault. I... Even though Professor prepared compressed air canisters for us, I didn't have it ready...and... It looked like I was going to be done in by Igniter's oxygen-deprivation attack, so Yumiko retreated. I'm sorry. I...made a mistake," finished Minoru with a weak smile on his face as he bowed his head in apology.

After Minoru did that, Olivier made a slight nod and smiled as well.

"Ah... I see. Gotcha. I mean, it happens, right? We all make mistakes," said Olivier, who then walked over to Minoru and patted his left shoulder.

Olivier then took his right hand off of Minoru's shoulder, raising it high as he clenched it into a fist...

Seconds later an explosive force crashed into Minoru's left cheek, and it sent him flying before he could even react. Minoru only realized that Olivier had punched him after he had been knocked back five meters and collided with the concrete wall. Minoru then slid down the wall and onto the floor.

This was the second time this month Minoru had been punched by someone. However, the first time was during the incident involving Tomomi Minowa when he was punched

by an upperclassman of the track club; he had subconsciously activated his shell, so he hadn't felt any pain.

It really hurts… Getting punched by someone…, he thought.

Not only did Minoru's cheek burn with throbbing pain, the pain was mixed with feelings of shame and helplessness that in turn would become a black liquid and flow into the swamp of his memories.

"Utsugi. Do you know why I sent you flying?" Olivier asked Minoru, slumped down on the floor.

"…It's because I made a mistake, right?" Minoru replied after a moment of silence.

"Nope.

"I told you, right? Everyone makes mistakes. I'm not criticizing you for that. The problem is that you're completely ignoring the fact that because of your mistake, someone died who didn't have to."

"…!" Minoru took a sudden sharp breath.

Olivier then walked past Minoru, his slippers clacking on the floor.

"Inside your head you think of it like it's someone else's problem, and that's because you lack resolve. You're not fit to be a member of the SFD, Utsugi. You should hurry up and get your Third Eye removed, your memory wiped, and go home," Olivier said, waving his left hand as he headed toward the elevator.

"You're wrong, Olivier," said Yumiko without getting up from her chair, in a quiet but firm voice, before Olivier could leave.

"Utsugi could have activated his shell before you punched him. If he had done that, right now your right hand would be broken in several places. At the very least, he had the resolve to take your punch."

Olivier paused and stood for a moment, but then disappeared into the elevator without answering.

*   *   *

A few minutes later.

DD and Yumiko had left and gone to the lower floors of the building, and in the experiment area at the west edge of the empty fifth-floor room, Minoru was being treated by Professor Riri Isa.

Minoru had protested, saying that he had only gotten a cut near the edge of his mouth and she didn't have to do anything, but Riri had forced Minoru into a chair, disinfected and bandaged his cut. After she finished and was uncharacteristically silent for a while, Riri finally spoke up.

"Uh…umm… Well, you see. About what Oli-V just said a minute ago…"

Minoru gave a wry smile and shook his head.

"It's fine. I don't plan on quitting the SFD," he said.

"I see." Riri smiled, looking relieved, and patted Minoru's arm. "I was having trouble thinking about how I would persuade you against doing so if you had told me you wanted to have your Third Eye extracted and memories erased… Geez, communicating with other people really is tough. There's never a clear-cut, single answer."

Riri the Speculator, who had the power to quickly find the answer to a problem if it existed, showed Minoru a bit of a childish smile, and she started to put up her first-aid kit.

With Riri's lab coat–wearing back turned toward Minoru, he said in a whisper, "…If I quit the SFD now and had Chief Himi erase my memories, including of what just happened, I didn't think that I could forget the feeling of that fist…"

"Well, then… Hmm… Yes, I suppose you're right," said Riri who turned around to look at Minoru and tilted her head in thought.

"When I was in second grade, I got into a stupid fight with a friend I had since kindergarten. I still clearly remember the pain of the slap she gave me."

"Wait...what?" Minoru cried out, unable to contain his surprise. "Professor, you got into a fight? You?"

"Now look here," said Riri, a cynical smile on her young face. "Up until three months ago, I was as much of a kid as I looked. Every day I did tons of stupid things, got angry and got others upset, cried and made others cry. That much is normal, right?"

"I...suppose so...," replied Minoru. When Riri put it that way, Minoru thought she made sense. Even before the incident eight years ago, Minoru had gotten into fights with his friends and his parents...and even with his older sister sometimes, and he had cried as well.

After Riri finished putting away the first-aid kit in its cabinet, she sat back down in front of Minoru on a stool.

"But really, even nowadays I think it's an experience that everyone needs to have," she said.

"You mean having a physical fight?" Minoru asked.

"Exactly. Ever since...I was infected by my Third Eye and obtained the power of speculation, I solved some questions that I really shouldn't have solved. Including, for instance, 'What is the meaning of life?'"

"Th-the meaning of life...?" asked Minoru, shocked, and stared at his strategic commander with braided hair. "Is there really an answer to that question...?"

"Of course there is. If there wasn't, what would be the point of philosophy or religion?" Riri replied.

"Wh-what is the answer...?" Minoru asked.

"It's a secret," said Riri, winking before putting a serious face back on. "However, due to finding that answer, while I can still 'think,' I have lost the human right to 'worry' or 'hesitate.'"

"The human right...?"

"Exactly. Mikkun, haven't you thought about it at least once before? Asked yourself why your worries will never end? During elementary school you might have been worried about a test, or a marathon event, about vaccine shots, or going to the dentist. When you grow up a little more, you worry about friendship and love, then later about going to college or finding work, about marriage and loans, about fighting disease... In life, there is never a point where all of your worries disappear, and that is because those worries are necessary."

"Is...worrying and hesitating really necessary?" asked Minoru.

"It is. The mental state of someone who does not worry is defective, just as mine is. So... After meeting you, I have felt a happiness rising from the bottom of my heart," Riri continued. "Your 'defensive shell' power is a huge mystery to me. You know, I am pretty sure that I have completely seen through why the red and black Third Eyes have fallen to Earth. However, after meeting you, I learned that one of the 'answers' that I have found was wrong. There is nothing more exciting to me than that.

"And that's because I realized...," Riri continued. "It might be possible that the answer I've found to the meaning of life is wrong as well. I believe...though this is just speculation, that your 'defensive shell' power is connected to the reason that Third Eyes exist. And that in turn is connected to the reason for all of human life to exist. Depending on a number of variables, it may be even connected to why the universe with its countless lives exists—"

"U-umm...," interrupted Minoru, as Riri had come so close to Minoru that their noses were almost touching.

Professor Riri blinked her eyes a few times, and then with her trademark cynical smile she pulled back.

"Oh, I'm sorry about that. I got a little carried away. ...Anyway, as you can probably tell, I'm interested in you. So I really don't want you to leave the SFD."

"Y-yes... I know. I won't quit, even if it's for a bit of a negative reason...," Minoru said, embarrassed that the only reason he could find for staying was that if he pulled out now, the memory of the pain of getting punched by Olivier would just continue to grow.

However, Professor Riri nodded with an all-encompassing smile on her face.

"All right, then. Worry yourself about it, Mikkun. Worry, hesitate, and when you need to, jump up in the air and scream in frustration!"

* * *

Even with Suka's willpower, he needed three hours to put the smoldering anger in the pit of his stomach to rest. Looking past the potted plants on his veranda, Suka watched as the winter sky darkened with every minute, repeatedly taking large breaths.

According to today's plan, Suka thought, after burning his prey in Shinjuku, he would easily evade the black hunters who would come after him until he got to a safe location. However, by making three mistakes, he was not only discovered, but also they saw his face, and he had let them get away.

Back then, instead of concentrating oxygen in the engine of the motorcycle and causing it to explode, he moved oxygen away from the motorcycle in order to asphyxiate the black riders. However, his oxygen-deprivation attack took time to have its full effect and there was nothing he could do to change that. Taking advantage of that opening, that young girl had used her power of acceleration to escape. He had no idea she would do something as outrageous as making the motorcycle leap up into the sky, vanishing from his sight in an instant.

Realizing that his breathing was getting shallower due to his anger and frustration, Suka attempted to breathe in more of the oxygen being produced from his plants and calm himself down.

"Fighting at close range is nothing short of barbaric," he said to himself, as he felt his anger finally cooling down.

Launching long-range combustion attacks was indicative of the true nature of his ability, and using that ability in that way was what fate wanted for him.

To raze this filthy civilization with cleaning flames.

That was why he had been given a new life.

Relaxing his arms and letting out a deep breath, Suka slowly looked to the side. On the wall of his unlit living room was a large detailed color map of the Tokyo metropolitan area.

On the map, the metal heads of pushpins gleamed red in the lingering light from the window. Suka walked over to the map and pulled out one pin out of extras he had set aside in the margins, and then pressed it in deep to mark the spot where today he had called forth his cleansing flames in West Shinjuku.

That one was the ninth.

Taking three steps back, Suka looked at the map. The orderly placed nine pins created a beautiful sign in the center of the sinful city that was Tokyo.

Soon those idiotic humans will realize, he thought, that this giant symbol would mark the beginning. It would mark the beginning of the divine punishment about to be inflicted on this polluted, overoxidized civilization.

"Heh-heh, heh-heh-heh," Suka chuckled, finally forgetting his anger, smiling with deep wrinkles on both sides of his mouth.

The fact that the black hunters had seen his face was certainly something to worry about, but there was no way that they would be able to track him to his apartment.

After all, Ayato Suka was completely and utterly dead.

* * *

"I'm sorry, Norie. We just can't seem to finish this group research project, and it's due tomorrow..."

"Hmm… Well, if that's the case, I suppose there's nothing else you can do. Make sure you thank the parents of the kid whose house you're staying at, okay? Also, even though it's to do homework, make sure you don't stay up too late."

"O-okay, I know… Tomorrow, I'll go straight to school from here."

"All right, roger that. Go and do your best okay?"

While feeling guilt for telling his adoptive sister such a bald-faced lie, Minoru took his smartphone away from his ear.

To be honest, Minoru had planned on returning to Saitama as soon as the meeting was over. However, after being punched by Olivier and talking to Professor Riri, he gave up on going home that day.

It wasn't that Minoru had suddenly become obstinate or stubborn, but at the very least he felt that he couldn't go home until he atoned in some way for his mistake.

However, there was only one thing that he could do right now and that was dig up the memories he had buried deep within his mind.

Sitting with his back to the wall and hugging his knees in the fifth-floor room of SFD Headquarters, Minoru closed his eyes to think.

He thought of Igniter's face, which he saw through the faceplate of his motorcycle helmet and the glass window of the taxi. Before it twisted with a raging intent to kill, it was a somewhat expressionless, teacherish face of a man who had begun to show his age.

It couldn't have possibly been that Minoru had just passed him by somewhere on the street. After all, Minoru never looked at the faces of people walking by. He was also sure that Igniter wasn't, for instance, a teacher who worked at his old elementary school or something like that, because if he remembered someone from back then, he would have recalled more than just the front of his expressionless face.

This was the only time that Minoru regretted his policy of acquiring as few memories as possible. Putting his chin on his knees, he pressed his fist against his forehead.

Just where did I...? he thought.

"...I don't think that there's any reason for you to feel this guilty about what happened."

Suddenly, Minoru heard a voice from above and immediately raised his head.

It was Yumiko, who had changed into slim jeans and a sweater, holding canned soft drinks in both of her hands.

Without looking straight at Minoru, Yumiko continued, stumbling along in her speech.

"Well, I mean...it's awful that the taxi driver died, but... not even Olivier is saying that you're to blame for that. Igniter is the one who killed him and the Third Eye that's infected him. Plus, the number of civilian casualties due to the actions of Ruby Eyes is easily more than a hundred, and that's only counting the data we've confirmed. If you plan to stay on as a member of the SFD... Though I really hate to say this...if you worry too much about each and every person sacrificed... it'll break you."

"...O-okay...," Minoru replied, nodding without looking up.

The only reason Minoru had his head in his hands was that he was trying to recall his memories, but he couldn't say that now and just took the canned soft drink that Yumiko offered to him. After a quick thank-you, he pulled the tab on the can and drank the cool soft drink, his thoughts still wandering absentmindedly.

Because of Minoru's mistake, that taxi driver, who otherwise wouldn't have been killed, became Igniter's newest victim. That was an undeniable fact. However, even though Minoru had been punched by Olivier and consoled by Yumiko, he didn't really feel any guilt at all.

Minoru thought back to what Professor Riri said before, *"The mental state of someone who does not worry is defective."*

Does that mean I'm abnormal? Minoru thought. *If so, is it because of my Third Eye? Or was I that way before?* But Minoru didn't get much further than that, as Yumiko sat down right beside him.

Skillfully opening the tab of the can with one hand and taking a gulp, Yumiko hesitantly turned to Minoru.

"Umm... About before... I'm sorry."

"Huh? Before? Do you mean during the meeting?" Minoru asked.

"No! I meant...on the roof...," Yumiko continued.

"The roof...," Minoru repeated before finally remembering what happened during his close call with death.

After being subjected to Igniter's oxygen-deprivation attack, Minoru was unable to breathe on his own, so Yumiko used her own lungs to provide the air to save Minoru. In other words, mouth-to-mouth...

Minoru leaned back and hit himself against the concrete wall, and Yumiko continued her hasty speech.

"I didn't have any other choice. If I had a manual resuscitator or something, I would have used that but had only prepared the motorcycle with light equipment... I'll make sure to have one next time."

"D-don't worry about it, I mean... If you didn't do that, I would have died," Minoru said.

"Well, then." Yumiko lightly nodded. "Let us both forget that that incident ever happened, okay? Especially the part where..."

"The part where you cried?" asked Minoru, remembering when Yumiko had hunched over with her shoulders shaking.

Yumiko glared at Minoru. "Yes, that. Now forget it. Right now."

"O-okay...," replied Minoru, nodding several times.

But just then, Minoru felt that stimulation of his memories again. He was surprised because this should have nothing to do with Igniter's face, but somewhere in his mind he was connecting that face with the act of artificial respiration.

"Artificial...respiration...," Minoru muttered, and Yumiko suddenly went red in the face.

"Didn't I just tell you to forget what happened?!" she yelled.

"Huh? Oh no, that's not what I meant. But I mean...isn't artificial respiration usually done on someone who was drowning? Instead, we did it on top of a tall building and...," said Minoru, trying to both make a proper excuse and gather his thoughts.

Artificial respiration was usually done when there was an accident in the water and someone was drowning... For example, if someone jumped into water on purpose, in order to...

"Th-that's it!!" Minoru yelled, jumping up, as Yumiko looked at him, startled.

But before Minoru could even notice Yumiko, in the back of his mind he saw Igniter's face, in black-and-white halftones. He hadn't seen him directly, he had seen a picture of him. A picture in a newspaper article.

"Are you sure this is him?" Riri asked.

Minoru stared at the low-resolution black-and-white photograph displayed on the eighty-inch monitor in front of him and nodded deeply.

"Yes, this is his face. This is Igniter."

As it was an enlarged photo from the digital version of a newspaper article, it wasn't very clear, but the looks of that intelligent-looking man and the signs of his age perfectly matched the person in Minoru's memories from just a few hours before.

"I see. Good work, Mikkun!" Riri said, vigorously turning

around before looking down at her tablet and summarizing the content of the newspaper article for Minoru and Yumiko.

"This man's name is Yousuke Nakakubo, and he is fifty-nine years old. His residence is located in Kaki-no-ki-zaka in the Meguro district of Tokyo, but...he probably doesn't live there anymore. Three months ago his landscaping company was faced with insolvency, and he attempted a murder-suicide with his wife. He drove his car off Ooi Pier and into the sea. However, when his car was pulled out of the water, only his wife and child's bodies were found. I guess this means he was alive."

"Three months ago...," Yumiko whispered, and Professor Riri nodded.

"Yes...it's quite the coincidence. However, it seems unlikely that he attempted suicide after he was infected by a Third Eye, as he would have to overthrow the Third Eye's will to do so. Which means...that he was probably infected after he escaped from the sinking car. That would explain his power as well."

"Huh...? What do you mean?" Minoru asked.

Riri lifted a finger and began to explain. "Third Eyes take their hosts' psychological state, their trauma or obsessions, their desires or attachments, and use them as a mold to create their supernatural powers. For example, in the case of gourmet Hikaru Takaesu, code name "Biter," he had been abused by his mother and lost more than half of his real teeth. Therefore, his Third Eye gave him a strong jaw and teeth that could bite through metal."

Riri then turned back around, looking up at the monitor, before continuing.

"The reason Igniter gained the frightening power to manipulate oxygen is not unrelated to the fact that he almost drowned. The fear and attachment to life and other psychological energy he must have felt in coming so close to death must have been enormous. Of all the Ruby Eyes that we have fought against and disposed of, not one had such an acute fear of death at the source of their power and that probably goes the same for us Jet Eyes."

Pausing for a moment, Riri turned back around.

The young strategic commander looked at both Minoru and Yumiko with her large eyes for an instant, but then looked down. Her cute voice was filled with a melancholy unfitting of her years.

"...In other words, if you just compare the strength of our powers, none of the forward-acting members of the SFD can match Igniter. This...may require us to bring Chief Himi along with us..."

When Minoru heard Himi's name mentioned, he blinked a few times. Chief Himi's power to seal other people's memories was certainly astounding, but what use would it have in battle? Minoru wondered.

However, Yumiko, who was next to Minoru, shook her head with a stern look on her face.

"No, that won't be necessary. I can deal with him alone," she said.

"But...," Riri started, her voice full of concern, but Yumiko, "Accelerator," cut her off.

"I'll be fine. Next time I'll take care of him for sure. ...I will go and investigate Igniter's residence. There may be clues there to his current hideout."

Yumiko then turned and walked quickly toward the elevator, her hair trailing behind her.

"Um... I'll go with her," Minoru said, quickly running after Yumiko as Riri told them to be careful.

When Yumiko and Minoru got off the elevator on the basement floor, they walked into the dim parking garage. Minoru saw the black minivan that he'd seen during the fight with Biter, as well as a small truck and Yumiko's motorcycle.

Taking a leather jacket off a hook on the concrete wall, Yumiko glanced back at Minoru. He thought that Yumiko would say something like, "I'm not bringing you along. You're just going to slow me down," but instead of saying anything, she just tossed him a helmet.

After Minoru put the helmet on, Yumiko also threw over a riding jacket with protective inserts, so Minoru took off his Chesterfield coat to put it on. This time, Minoru made sure he was equipped with his compressed air cylinder in his pocket, and after he finished doing so, Professor Riri's voice came in over the intercom.

"I'll send you Igniter's old address. I'm also currently checking for any information on his real name with the department of public safety, the police, and the fire department, but I don't expect to find much."

Immediately afterward, a full-color map was displayed on the right side of the helmet's faceplate, surprising Minoru. Apparently it was equipped with a clear display.

"...Thank you for letting me do this, Professor," said Yumiko in a small voice.

"Don't do anything rash. If I run across any new information I'll contact you immediately," replied Riri before ending the transmission.

Even though it was only just past five o'clock in the afternoon, Shinjuku had already taken on its night landscape. Under bright neon lights, the motorcycle Yumiko and Minoru were riding raced at just under the legal speed limit.

The map on the right side of Minoru's helmet faceplate displayed the route to Kaki-no-ki-zaka in Meguro. Yumiko, who had taken Meiji Street south all the way to Ebisu, turned right onto Komazawa Street and flitted back and forth through traffic.

Given her skill at riding, Minoru thought that Yumiko had been riding motorcycles since before she got her Third Eye, but Minoru thought that in order to get a motorcycle license, you had to be at least sixteen years old. Since Yumiko said that she was a first-year high school student, just like Minoru, she might have at most just turned sixteen a few months ago. But even considering that...

"...Umm," said Minoru over the intercom.

"What is it?" Yumiko asked.

"What was the engine size of this motorcycle again?"

"It's 798cc," Yumiko replied.

"Which means it counts as a large-model motorcycle, right?"

"That's correct."

"What was the earliest age that you could get a large-model motorcycle license again?"

"Eighteen, of course," said Yumiko tersely, before pulling hard on the accelerator.

Minoru, who was about to yell out, "What?!" had his outcry shoved back down his throat as he was subjected to the g-force of the acceleration.

About ten minutes later, after entering a residential area and returning to modest speeds, they stopped in front of a single house.

After confirming that they had reached their destination on the map, Minoru let out a sigh. "That's a really big house."

"You would think that the land alone would go for more than a hundred million yen," replied Yumiko, with a little bit of shock in her voice as well.

The residence, which was surrounded by a tall rock-wall fence, had to be at least three hundred square meters, but there were lots of fallen leaves scattered in the yard and there was a large sign in the front that marked the house for sale.

After pulling the motorcycle around the back and shutting off the engine, Yumiko got off the motorcycle and looked up at the tall rock-wall fence.

"We're going to jump. Don't take off your helmet. It'll be a lot of trouble if our faces got caught on a security camera."

"What do you mean by...jump?" Minoru asked.

"Exactly how it's written in the dictionary," she said, wrapping her arm around Minoru's waist.

After a short dip down, she kicked off the ground.

Acceleration.

With one jump they landed on top of the fence, and with another jump they leaped onto the roof.

After Yumiko released Minoru, she added unaffectedly, "With my own jump power, that's about all I can do. It's a lot more fun to use the motorcycle."

"I...think I've had more than my share of enjoyment of that," Minoru replied, shaking his head. *What are we, ninjas in a B action movie?* he thought, but didn't say anything more.

From the roof they descended to a second-floor veranda, and Yumiko cut a hole in the glass from a strange tool she took out of her pocket and unlocked the door. From there, they entered the house. The first room they entered appeared to be a ten tatami mat–size bedroom, but the panels of the double bed were sticking out and the walk-in closet was also empty.

Yumiko clicked her tongue and opened the faceplate of her helmet, whispering in a thick voice. "It looks like they've already completely cleaned this place out... Hey, what are you doing?"

Minoru, who had been earnestly sniffing the air as soon as they entered the house, raised the faceplate on his helmet as well to answer.

"What if Igniter's lying in wait somewhere for us here? I wanted to check to see if I could smell the scent of a Ruby Eye..."

"Look here, this house is already up for sale. There are interested buyers who are going to come to see the inside of the house, so there's no way he'd be hiding out here."

"Well, I suppose that may be true, but..." Minoru nodded before taking another deep breath of air, making sure he could not smell that primordial beast–like smell of the Ruby Eyes.

"Once you're satisfied, meet me down on the first floor. If there's a study that Igniter...that Nakakubo used, we might be able to find a clue there," said Yumiko.

"Umm... I don't smell any Ruby Eyes, but...don't you smell something else? Even though it looks like it's been cleaned, there's still this smell."

"Really?" asked Yumiko, making sniffing motions with her well-formed nose before grimacing. "...You're right. I wonder what it is..."

"It reminds me of...a wet rag," Minoru said.

"Do you think that one of the cleaning staff just left a mop out?"

They continued their conversation as they opened the door and headed down to the first floor. The hallway was only lit by a small amount of light from the outside and was almost completely submerged in darkness. The damp smell grew stronger, and Minoru started to feel uneasy.

"U-umm... Yumiko?"

When they reached the end of the hall and Yumiko started to walk down the stairs, Minoru grabbed the sleeve of Yumiko's leather jacket.

"What is it?"

"...Aren't you scared?" Minoru asked.

"Of what?"

"Of... I don't know...ghosts or monsters?"

As soon as Yumiko heard those words, she looked at Minoru as if he were stupid and started to walk away when he grabbed her sleeve again.

"Now look here!"

"B-but...the family who lived here was killed in a murder-suicide, right? And now we're breaking in, in the middle of the night. Doesn't this completely follow the sort of pattern where they appear?" Minoru said.

It wasn't as if Minoru truly believed in ghosts, but despite the fact that he was uncontrollably nervous, Yumiko seemed just fine, so he couldn't help but say something. But Yumiko didn't flinch.

"Of course they're not going to appear. Ghosts and stuff don't exist."

"Well...Third Eyes exist, right? And they're these mysterious objects from outer space. Plus, they're parasitic and infect humans. I mean, when things like that exist, can you show any proof that ghosts don't?"

"...I don't know what you're getting at," she said, lifting her beautiful eyebrows high. "But what? Are you trying to scare me? I hate to break it to you, but if a ghost pops out, I'll just accelerate my way out of here, so I have nothing to be afraid of."

"...That's so unfair."

"You have your defensive shell, don't you? Not that I know if it can block out ghosts," added Yumiko, before walking off again, not wanting to deal with Minoru anymore, who had no choice but to chase after her.

Since all of the windows on the first floor were shuttered with antitheft panels, it was completely dark. Yumiko took a small LED flashlight out of her pocket and the white light lit the hall.

"I wonder if this was his study. It would be nice if a computer or some documents were left...," Yumiko muttered and opened the door. Inside was a writing desk, cabinets, and shelves, but unfortunately, everything was empty.

Yumiko let out a disappointed sigh as she walked into the room, but immediately held her hand to her nose as soon as she did.

"...This smell..."

Minoru, who walked into the room after her, almost choked on the thick stench that permeated the room.

The smell of wet rags that they sensed on the second floor was much stronger in this room. However, there was no abandoned mop in the room as Yumiko predicted.

As they searched the room for the source of the smell, they found a large air purifier in the corner of the room. It appeared brand-new and must have been set up recently.

"I wonder if the reason this house hasn't sold in three months is due to this smell. The real-estate management must have put in the air purifier. It doesn't look like it's doing any good, though," Yumiko muttered, her hand over her nose as she started to search the cabinets of the desk.

Minoru also went and opened up the glass cabinets, for lack of anything better to do, but it was clear that they were empty.

A few minutes later, they were still continuing their fruitless search.

"…Umm," said Minoru.

"Did you find anything?" asked Yumiko, turning around, but Minoru just shook his head.

"No, I haven't found anything, but…don't you hear something?" asked Minoru.

Though she had a suspicious look on her face, Yumiko paused to listen.

Given that it was such a luxurious residence, the sound seemed to be fairly insulated from room to room, and they could hardly hear any sounds from outside the room. But in the middle of that deafening silence…

…*Drip.*

…was the quiet sound of a water droplet.

Minoru and Yumiko looked at each other, their faces both stiffening at the same time.

Drop.

Yumiko suddenly jumped as if she had used her power. She ran behind Minoru and clutched his shoulders.

"Wh-what are you doing?" Minoru asked in a raspy voice, but Yumiko quickly answered back.

"What's the problem?! You've got your shell, right? But who cares about that, what is that sound?! Where is it coming from?!"

"...It sounds like water dripping, but... I wonder if there's a leaky faucet somewhere," Minoru said.

"That can't be it, this house is for sale! They should have shut off the gas and the water," Yumiko replied.

"...Oh...that makes sense," said Minoru, listening for the sound once more.

Drip.

Drop.

The sound that Minoru thought couldn't possibly be any other sound than droplets falling into a pool of water sounded at regular intervals, but Minoru still couldn't figure out where they were coming from. The sounds themselves were something that someone without the enhanced senses of a Third Eye host would miss, so they were very, very quiet.

Forgetting the rotten smell, Minoru focused all of his senses on the sound of the water. He wasn't listening with his ears, but rather feeling the sound's vibrations in the air with his entire body.

Drip.

"...It's coming from underneath us," Minoru whispered, and with Yumiko still clinging to his back, he walked in front of the giant mahogany desk in the room.

If there was a route from this room leading underground, then this desk would be the only way to hide it.

Minoru grabbed the top edge of the reddish-brown desk and put a little bit of his strength into it. It was heavy. The desk seemed to be made of solid wood, instead of wood paneling over cheaper materials. However, it wasn't so heavy that a Third Eye host's strength couldn't move it.

Bending down and using his legs, Minoru lifted the edge of the desk a few centimeters off the ground and rotated it ninety degrees, using the leg on the far edge as a pivot.

"There...," Yumiko said from behind Minoru.

A small hatch had appeared in a spot that was hidden directly under the desk. The floorboards were cut out in a rectangular shape and there was a metal handle to pull the hatch open.

As Minoru put his face closer to the hatch, both the terrible smell and the sound of the water became clearer.

"...Good job finding something terribly unpleasant," whined Yumiko.

"...Should we pretend we didn't see anything?" asked Minoru, but after a few seconds, Yumiko let out a sigh.

"Well, we can't really do that...can we? All right, let's open it. Be on your guard."

"Got it." Minoru nodded, and after making sure there were no security cameras, he took off his helmet and gave it to Yumiko.

Minoru grabbed the handle and pulled the hatch open. From the darkness under the hatch, an unbearable stench rose and Minoru held his breath. It was the smell of mold and foul water. This was undoubtedly the source of the smell drifting throughout the house.

Yumiko also took off her helmet, and holding her nose with her left hand, she pointed her LED light down the hatch

A steep set of stairs led almost straight down the hatch, and at a certain point, the white light reflected back. Water. The hidden basement was completely flooded.

"What...is this?" muttered Yumiko, moving the light around. However, the muddy water just reflected the light back, and it was impossible to tell what it was like under the surface.

At least it was certain that this was not a place that someone could be hiding. There was only about one meter between the opening of the hatch and the surface of the water. The wooden steps were covered in black mold and had partially rotted. The sound of the water came from moisture that had condensed on the basement ceiling that was now falling back down in droplets.

"...Hey, Utsugi?" Yumiko whispered to Minoru before the next droplet fell.

"...What is it?"

"It...was my first time."

"...What was?"

"That kiss."

Minoru, sensing Yumiko's intent behind that incredibly straight statement, rushed to object.

"That doesn't count; it was an emergency, a life-or-death situation...and didn't you say not too long ago for me to forget everything?"

"A maiden's heart is not that clear-cut," Yumiko said.

Here, Minoru had to hold himself in and somehow was able to keep from arguing back, "What kind of 'maiden' rides around on an 800cc motorcycle and hides a stun baton in her skirt?!"

Instead, he drooped his head.

"...All right, I'll go."

When he did, Yumiko, at least on the surface, showed an innocent smile and whispered, "I knew you would say that, I believed in you! I knew I could trust the one I gave my first kiss t—"

"That's enough! Now give me that light," Minoru said, cutting her off and snatching her LED light before letting out a sigh.

"...When I activate my shell, we won't be able to communicate. If something happens to me down there, I'll signal you by flashing this light."

"Understood. If that happens I'll call someone to help you," Yumiko said.

"..." Minoru paused, unsure how serious Yumiko was, looking at her smile out of the corner of his eye.

...It was my first time, too, you know? he muttered to himself inside his head.

After taking a deep breath away from that hatch to minimize breathing in the stench, Minoru held his breath and activated his shell.

The silence that fell around Minoru was enough of a difference that it made him realize that even that quiet mansion had been filled with various sounds.

However, immediately after, he heard a low-pitched *dunn, dunn* sound. It was always there when he activated his shell, but Minoru still had no idea where it was coming from.

Minoru pointed the LED light down, which he had held firmly in his hand so it wouldn't be ejected, and after finding his determination, he headed down the steep stairs.

In the blue-tinted light Minoru saw from inside his shell, the steps looked very slippery. However, Minoru was able to firmly plant his feet on the steps through his shell.

On the fourth step, he sunk his left foot into the water. Confirming that his shell repelled the murky water, Minoru carefully continued walking into the basement. The water level reached his waist, then his chest, and then up to his neck. Even when he was completely submerged, Minoru strangely didn't feel any buoyancy. Rather than sinking into the water, Minoru felt that he was passing in between the water particles and continued down into the water.

The steps went farther down than Minoru had expected. When Minoru finally reached the bottom, he thought that he had come five meters under the floor. The murkiness of the water had only worsened and blocked the light of the high-brightness LED light. Minoru carefully advanced with his arm outstretched in front of him.

After a few steps forward, a wooden shelf-like object appeared in front of him. However, the spacing between the compartments looked too small to hold books. Each compartment was square, about ten centimeters for each side, and there were several of them. After finding some old-looking glass bottles in some of the compartments, Minoru finally realized what this basement was used for.

It was a wine cellar. Since wine was weak to changes in temperature and to light, Minoru had read somewhere that it was sometimes stored underground like this. However, there wasn't much wine left on the shelf. A lot of the wine must have been sold to help pay down debt. Minoru understood that, but why...?

Why was it flooded?

Did some underground water seep through the walls? But if this was a wine cellar, they must have taken several measures to waterproof the cellar and prevent that from happening. To look at it another way, that was probably a reason why the water hadn't drained out.

Looking for clues, Minoru shined the LED light in all directions. The answer was close by, sunk on the floor.

There was a bright blue curving line. It was a sprinkling hose, coiled up like a snake. Someone must have connected one end to a nearby sink on the first floor to intentionally flood the cellar.

He had no idea how many thousands of liters it would take to submerge this cellar, but someone intentionally pumped in enough water for it to reach the roof.

However, Minoru still couldn't figure out a reason.

Why would the owner of this cellar, why would Igniter, do something like that?

In order to flood the basement, it was necessary to use the water line, so he had to have done it at least three months ago before the water was shut off. Then, was it before Igniter became a Ruby Eye? When he was Yousuke Nakakubo, president of a landscaping company?

As Minoru stood lost in thought in the water, he felt someone from behind tap him on his right shoulder.

"I'm sorry, could you give me a minute?" Minoru said and continued to think. After Nakakubo flooded his wine cellar, he had hidden the hatch with his desk and attempted to commit murder-suicide with his family.

Still, Minoru couldn't think of any logical reason someone about to commit suicide would do something like that.

Then did he do it after he became Igniter? If it was immediately after his disppearance, the water may still have been running.

Again, Minoru was tapped on his shoulder.

"Like I said before, I'm in the middle of...," Minoru started to say and then paused.

... *Wait, what?*

Minoru froze.

It couldn't possibly be Yumiko. Minoru was currently four meters underwater.

"..."

Gulping, with his eyes open wide, Minoru slowly turned around.

What he saw, shining in his LED light, was the stark-white, bloated face of a corpse.

Ashen eyes buried within the bloated skin of a face stared at Minoru, right in front of him.

"Gyahh!!" went the sound of Minoru's scream as it echoed within his shell.

11

Holding in both hands the mug of café au lait that Yumiko had poured for him, Minoru finally had returned to a normal state of mind and let out a deep breath that had been tied up in his chest.

After returning to SFD Headquarters, he had used the shower in his room, 403, but the chill he had felt sinking deep into the marrow of his bones just would not go away. Naturally, Minoru had carried, through his shell, the corpse that he had found in the basement up to the first floor; deactivated his shell and taken pictures, fingerprints; and searched the pockets of its shirt and pants.

Given the fact that during that entire time, Yumiko had cowered outside of the room, a café au lait was not enough to properly thank him.

As Minoru sipped the drink, a little too sweet for his tastes, he had kept his gaze fixed right beside him, but Yumiko continued to ignore him and instead looked at the monitor Professor Riri was working on.

"...Bingo!" Riri said, snapping her fingers.

Riri had run the corpse's fingerprints through the police's AFIS (Automated Fingerprint Identification System) fingerprint database, and there was a match. Minoru took his gaze off of Yumiko and looked at the monitor.

Displayed on the screen was the face of a relatively good-looking young man.

"Wait, that corpse...was this man?" Minoru asked, and Riri nodded.

"There's no mistaking it. The corpse had begun to swell and the face has changed considerably, but not only do their fingerprints match, the shape of their ears is also the same. Due to the fact that the corpse was held in cold water for a long time, it seems that it grayed without rotting."

Holding in the feeling of disconnect Minoru felt from hearing a cute fourth grader's voice explain the state of a corpse, Minoru asked another question.

"But then... Who is it?"

"He was a man who worked as an accountant for Nakakubo Green Earth, Igniter's landscaping company. His name is Ayato Suka, and he was twenty-nine years old," Riri replied.

"Does this mean that Igniter killed his own employee?"

"Exactly. Suka was fired from the company eight months ago and at the same time was sued for fraud. He was accused of taking ten million yen from the company, and this is why his fingerprint came up in the AFIS database. However, possibly due to the skills of his lawyer, he had his sentence suspended. If Suka was the reason Nakakubo Green Earth went bankrupt, that should provide an adequate reason for Nakakubo, the president of the company, to hate him."

As Riri continued with her explanation, she made several clicks with her mouse and opened a new window on the screen. Now she seemed to be looking at data from Japan's Basic Resident Registry Network System.

"Suka was single, and his parents were both already deceased. There wasn't even a missing person's report filed. ...So I suppose this means that after Igniter recovered from nearly dying, he killed Suka in revenge and hid the body in the basement of his residence..."

"But then, does that mean that there's no information connecting these events to where Igniter is now?" asked Yumiko in a dejected voice.

Minoru was also disappointed. Even though he had to go through such a frightening experience, it felt unfair that they uncovered zero clues. However, Minoru quickly caught himself, telling himself that it wasn't completely in vain.

No matter what the reason he was killed, this man Suka was still a victim of Igniter. There was meaning simply in the fact that his hidden corpse was found, Minoru thought. There was no way his soul would be able to properly leave this world if he was stuck, sunk in that deep, dark water...

"Water...," Minoru muttered, and Yumiko and Professor Riri both looked at him suspiciously.

"Is there something that caught your attention, Mikkun?" Riri asked.

"Ah no, it's nothing particularly important, but I was just wondering why it was water this time and not fire. Other than the taxi driver, all of Igniter's victims were burned to death, right?"

"That is certainly correct...," said Riri; tilting her head in thought, she immediately had an answer.

"I think it's safe to say that he wanted to hide the corpse. In terms of kerosene, the amount of fuel necessary to completely burn a person away is about eighty liters. It's very hard to keep a giant flame like that out of sight from witnesses in an urban place like Tokyo. There's also the issue of smoke... Unlike Biter, Igniter has never seemed to make an effort to hide his actions. But that begs the question. Why did he want to hide Suka's corpse...?"

Riri, in her lab coat, crossed her arms and closed her eyes.

After a single second, her eyes popped open with such a force that Minoru almost expected them to make a sound, and Riri declared, "His reason for killing Suka was not simply out of revenge, nor was it a demonstration."

"Huh?" Minoru asked.

"What do you mean?" Yumiko responded as well.

With her back turned to Minoru and Yumiko, Professor Riri make more clicks with her mouse.

What was then displayed on the screen was, astonishingly, an electric company's customer data. Apparently the SFD was not subject to privacy laws. After making a quick search through the giant list, Riri snapped her fingers again.

"Just as I thought. Suka, who should have been killed, is still paying his monthly electric bills and not on any automatic payment program. He's just paying monthly at convenience stores."

"What?! But Suka died months ago...," Minoru started to say before he finally realized what Professor Riri was trying to say. "...Do you mean that the one paying the electric bill now is...?"

"Exactly. It's Igniter. Igniter, aka Nakakubo, killed Suka; hid his corpse; and took on his identity," Riri explained.

After a few seconds of silence, Yumiko spoke up.

"But...is it really that easy to do something like that?"

"No. However, Suka was single, detained by the police, and the company he worked at dissolved. In other words his social environment was reset. If you can fake your age and have a new ID card issued, it's not impossible to take on someone else's identity in that case."

After searching again through the Basic Resident Registry Network System, as well as a number of other databases, Riri spoke up again with strong conviction in her voice.

"Just as I thought. Three months ago, there are signs that he filed for a new resident card. And... Well, this is surprising... According to this credit card company's data, he seems to be employed, working at a company called Ariake Heaven's Shore... Now what could that be?"

"Wait, you mean you don't know?" said Yumiko, surprised.

"I bet all of the kids at my school know. It's a big water park that's set to open this year. It's completely indoors, so you can experience an endless summer, even in the winter...," Yumiko continued.

"Well, I'm sorry for not knowing," Riri retorted in her cute voice, pouting. "Publicly, I'm a problem child who's quit going to school. Not too long ago I received a ton of letters from the kids in my class telling me to 'Get better soon and come back to school.' If you'd like, I could read them out to you. How about it?"

"N-no thanks…," said Yumiko, shaking her head back and forth.

Having received letters like that himself, Minoru felt a cold sweat coming on, just imagining what was written in them.

"Putting that issue aside, we've discovered Igniter's current address, correct?" Yumiko continued.

"Yes. There is an apartment in Toyosu in Tokyo's Koto district being rented in Suka's name, but…I think it would be very risky to just rush into his apartment…"

"Risky?" Minoru asked, tilting his head.

"It's very common for Ruby Eyes to have something prepared at their hideouts in case they are attacked. But of course, I mean, we do the same thing," Yumiko replied.

"Huh? What sort of…preparations do we have at headquarters?"

"You'll find out soon enough. Anyway, in a worst-case scenario the entire apartment building might go up in flames. At the very least, we're at a disadvantage because Igniter's power is effective at range," continued Yumiko.

"Therefore," said Riri, picking up Yumiko's explanation, "it's best to target him when he's on the move. We can observe him from afar and, if possible, attack him where there are few people around, but that's no simple task, either… No, wait a minute."

With Riri controlling it, the content of the windows on the screen flitted back and forth. This time it appeared that she had broken into the network of the company that Igniter was working at.

"Igniter, under the name of Ayato Suka, was hired at this Ariake Heaven's something or another theme park to work as a janitor. His work time is from eight a.m. to four p.m. from Wednesday to Sunday, and on Monday it is from ten p.m. to six a.m. the next morning. Today is Monday, so he should be working the night shift tonight. At that time, there should only be a small number of security guards and janitors inside the park."

"Then it's settled," Yumiko said, gripping her right hand into a fist, and Riri nodded.

"Tonight, we'll storm Igniter's workplace. I'll infiltrate the security camera system and use it to pinpoint Igniter's location. When he's alone, we will surround him and quickly disable him. We'll start our operation at one a.m. Participating members will be Yumiko, DD, Oli-V—"

"I-I'll go, too," Minoru interrupted, dismissing the fears he had about Igniter's oxygen-deprivation attack.

Both Riri and Yumiko looked at Minoru for a moment, and then both nodded.

"All right. If that's the case, first we should all eat a solid dinner," Riri said.

"But if we get DD to start making dinner now, we won't have time to rest before the operation... But I'm not sure frozen pizza will do much for our fighting spirits...," Yumiko said, and both silently stared at Minoru.

"...A-all right, I'll do it, but I make no guarantees about the flavor, okay?" Minoru replied, getting the feeling that his position at the SFD was settling down in an unsatisfactory way.

Moving toward the kitchen on the other side of the large room, he felt a clump of anxiety in his chest, like he was missing something important.

The way Igniter's face looked that day, when Minoru clearly saw him in Ikebukuro, that sunken mold-filled basement, and the fact that he was employed at a theme park just didn't seem to match up. It was as if the edges of the pieces in a jigsaw puzzle were just slightly off.

However, when Minoru opened the German-made refrigerator, he had his eyes taken away by the overflowing fresh ingredients and quickly forgot his anxiety. It looked like DD had just refilled the refrigerator, so Minoru set to work matching what ingredients were available with his repertoire of recipes.

If I'm looking for a recipe that's simple to make and can give you energy, it'll have to be Chinese-style fried rice, thought Minoru. *I'll top it with a ton of vegetables in a sauce and add in egg drop soup on the side.*

As Minoru took out onions, carrots, and filleted pork, he concentrated on his recipe.

* * *

The man who was sometimes Ayato Suka, Yousuke Nakakubo, and occasionally Igniter looked satisfied at the shine of the glass he had just polished clean and hopped off his stepladder.

After landing firmly on the tile floor, he took his basket of cleaning supplies in his right hand and five-step ladder in his left and moved to the next pane of glass.

From the bottom right corner, he sprayed the foamy cleaner and used a microfiber cloth to carefully wipe it away. The building was silent, in stark contrast to the hustle and bustle of the day, and only the squeaking of him polishing the glass could be heard.

Many of his collegues hated the special cleaning that went on during the Monday midnight shift, but Nakakubo didn't dislike it.

Nakakubo, who used to manage the exterior design of large mansions and businesses as a first-rate landscaper, now called himself by the lowly name of Ayato Suka, and as he crawled around this theme park cleaning glass, he couldn't help but feel a little self-scorn. However, ever since he was infected by this sphere in his right hand, he could hardly remember anything about when he'd been a landscaper.

Nakakubo had always liked cleanliness and didn't hate

to clean, and as his body was tempered by his Third Eye, no matter how he pushed himself, he didn't feel any soreness. Additionally, this name and identity he was using was only temporary. In actuality, Nakakubo was not a theme park janitor, but a cleanser of polluted human civilization. If he thought of it that way, it wasn't exactly unfitting for him to be doing work like this.

A wrinkly smile on his thin face, Nakakubo took one step back and looked at the glass he had just polished, regarding himself in the glossy reflection as if it were a mirror.

He had lived with the name Nakakubo for fifty-nine years, and when he was reborn, he took on the name Suka and was called Igniter by both the red organization and the black hunters. However, in the near future, when his power reached its next stage, everyone would call him by a more fitting name: "Purifier."

"Heh... Heh-heh," he chuckled in a deep voice, imagining the new world that was to come.

That day was near. In order to further evolve his already advanced power to manipulate oxygen, he had picked this place of work. Here, there were vast amounts of oxygen for him to resonate with, and in a high concentration.

One day, he would free all beautiful and proud of the elements of the sixteenth group from humanity's filthy hands.

He would keep the savages from performing any oxidation whatsoever.

Heat-powered electric generation? NO.

Gasoline engines? NO.

Garbage incineration? Gas heaters? Cigarettes? NO, NO, NO.

Breathing?

"...That, too, of course, NO," he said, chuckling to himself as he returned to polishing the glass, stepping up his ladder, and wiping away the smudges from the top corner.

As he continued his simple work, his exhilaration faded and a faint worry popped up in the corner of his mind.

His face had been seen by one of the black hunters.

Was that enough to unravel his lifestyle of disguise? After he had attempted murder-suicide, the newspaper had put one picture of his face in the newspaper. If that black hunter had read that article and remembered the picture, it would be possible for him to track down the name Yousuke Nakakubo.

If they did that, they might go snooping around his house in Meguro. They might find the entrance to his wine cellar he hid under his desk, and if they investigated under the water, they might even find the real Ayato Suka's corpse.

Was it careless of him to have left the corpse in his own house?

However, Nakakubo couldn't bear to only kill that lowly idiot of a traitor. Even with the level of power he had had then, if he had taken enough time, he could have burned away the body.

However, if he had done that in that high-population density of an area, he wouldn't have been able to hide the flames or the smell, and since he had lost his car after driving it off Ooi Pier, he had no way to transport the corpse, either.

Therefore, in order to give that filth a proper cleansing, he sealed the body deep underwater.

It would be soon. If he could just break through one thin layer still holding him back, he would reach a new stage of his power. Nakakubo could feel it right now, the wills of the large amount of oxygen wishing to join his cause.

It wasn't a problem. This disguise should hold for just a little while longer, Nakakubo thought.

Even if they found the body, they shouldn't be able to immediately realize that Ayato Suka, who should have died, was still out walking around. All he needed was one more week. One more week and he would have burned the number of humans he had originally planned and drawn his sign of purification in the city.

Then, he would evolve. He would awaken to his true power.

Nakakubo shook off his anxiety and laughed in a deep voice once again, and that laugh soon changed into a hum as he sang, "Oxygen... Oxygen..."

* * *

Minoru was only able to get three hours of sleep in after dinner, but by the time his smartphone alarm woke him up, he felt completely rested.

While Minoru waited for the other members in SFD Headquarters' underground parking garage, he ran his fingers along the bandage at the edge of his mouth. His body felt light and his mind was clear, but he could still feel a little bit of pain left, and the memory that went along with that pain unfortunately had not disappeared, either.

At dinner, Minoru wasn't able to look Olivier Saito in the eye. Olivier, on the other hand, didn't seem to care at all about what happened during the day and had wolfed down the fried rice Minoru had prepared at an incredible pace and also made fun of DD, who seemed as if he had been one-upped somehow.

Yumiko, who sat next to Minoru, whispered to him to forget about the whole thing, but Minoru just didn't have the courage to do so.

In the end, Minoru didn't say a single word to Olivier throughout the whole meal, so was unable to apologize and was still worrying about the incident now, even as they were just about to head off on their mission.

Inside your head you think of it like it's someone else's problem, and that's because you lack resolve.

It wasn't just the pain of the punch—Minoru also could remember Olivier's words very clearly.

Minoru knew that he lacked resolve. He didn't join the SFD because he wanted to protect anyone or any righteous cause like that. He joined because of a very selfish reason, because he wanted Chief Himi to use his power to erase himself from the memories of everyone around him.

However, the words *You think of it like it's someone else's problem* cut deep into his heart.

Was there even once that Minoru seriously thought to use the power he received as a Jet Eye to save anyone or protect anyone? Minoru asked himself, and the answer to that question was most probably no.

Even the time when Minoru had tried to protect Tomomi Minowa when she was attacked by Biter or tried to save Norie when she was kidnapped, he felt that the majority of his motivation was that he just didn't want to have to go through experiencing that happening from *his* perspective.

It was no different from that time in the convenience store when Minoru put on an act to help an elementary school kid who didn't have enough money at the register. In the end, Minoru was only doing it for himself, simply because he didn't want to have to muddy his memories with regret.

So Minoru couldn't save anyone. So long as it wasn't directly his fault, he didn't care. That was just the kind of person he was.

Even after Minoru was punched by Olivier, somewhere in his heart he kept thinking, *Igniter was the one who killed that taxi driver. It's not my fault.*

If that's the case, then is that incident really not your fault as well? Minoru heard a voice asking him.

When your mother and father...and your older sister Wakaba were killed, are you really not at fault for doing nothing, and hiding away, shaking under the floor? the voice asked.

Leaning back against the cold concrete wall of the parking garage, Minoru desperately argued back.

I was only a second grader in elementary school! It was all I could do just to hide! My sister told me that it was going to be okay. So I had to keep counting, even when those frightening footsteps came, I kept counting and counting and counting and...

"...Uwaaaahhh!!" Minoru yelled out in a suppressed voice and forcibly cut off his train of thought. A switch flipped in the back of his mind and fell into an empty darkness.

Minoru only realized that he had unconsciously activated his defensive shell when that strange low-frequency sound met his ears. It didn't sound like it was mechanical or organic. The air had no scent and the light, no color. It was a world without anyone in it.

Minoru huddled in the shadow of a concrete pillar and hugged his knees.

But right before he closed his eyes, he saw mid-cut sneakers right in front of him on the floor.

When Minoru raised his head, there was Yumiko, who had changed out of her riding jacket and into her blazer uniform, standing with a harsh light in her eyes. Her lips moved, and even though Minoru couldn't hear her, he could tell what she was saying.

"Come out of your shell."

"...I don't want to," Minoru said inside of the shell and tried to look back down.

But when he did, Yumiko crouched down right in front of him, gripped her slender right hand into a fist, and lifted it in the air, aiming for Minoru's left cheek.

Smack.

Minoru felt a strong force run through his right cheek. Yumiko's arm had swung all the way through the punch and stopped. It was such a forceful punch that he could hear the grinding of her shoulder and elbow.

"Wha…," groaned Minoru before railing at Yumiko. "What were you thinking?! If I had been a second later in deactivating my shell, right now your…"

"My right hand would have been broken. But that didn't happen, did it?" Yumiko smiled and touched Minoru's cheek with her open hand. She looked into Minoru's eyes, which had opened wide, and whispered from a close distance, "You know, Utsugi? Before, you asked me if I really knew what it meant to be hated, right?"

"Well…yeah."

"Well, the answer is yes. I know. I know what it means to be hated," Yumiko said.

While the expression on her face was normal, the tone of her voice was tense and like steel. In front of Minoru, who couldn't find any words to say, Yumiko suddenly lifted up her skirt. She lifted it up high enough so that the tops of the knee-high stockings she always wore with her uniform were exposed. In even the dim light of the parking garage, her white thighs shined bright, and Minoru quickly tried to look away, but at that moment…

"Look," Yumiko whispered and pulled the stocking on her right leg down to her ankle.

"…!!" Minoru took a breath in shock.

Underneath Yumiko's well-shaped knee was a frightfully long, large scar. Minoru could see the keloid scar tissue and traces of where stitches ran across it.

"You see, before I became a Jet Eye, I couldn't even walk without a crutch," Yumiko said, still smiling. "The ones who gave me this scar were the upperclassmen of my middle school track team. With wooden swords and metal pipes, they hit me until they shattered my knee. Their reason for doing so was because I was faster than them and had a bad attitude, apparently. They did it for only that reason."

Being disliked was far too gentle to describe what had happened to her. Minoru felt that the incredible intensity of the hatred that Yumiko took on with her body exuded from every stitch mark.

Minoru, who had been running on the banks of the Arakawa River for five years, knew. He knew how precious a treasure a runner's legs were to them. Legs that they had spent years training and refining. Even a small injury is enough to cause anxiety over whether it will properly heal…

"…How?" Minoru asked in a raspy voice.

"Hmm?"

"How can you still believe in other people after this horrible thing has happened to you?" Minoru asked in a raspy voice. "How could you believe that I would deactivate my shell just now? There was no way you could have known for sure."

Yumiko didn't say anything for a while. She wordlessly pulled her stocking back up to its original position and smoothed out her skirt before sitting down, hugging her knees in front of Minoru.

With their eyes on the same level, Yumiko finally said, "Because you're not 'just someone else' to me anymore."

Minoru looked down to avert his eyes from Yumiko's strong, bright gaze.

"…I don't understand. I can't understand. I… I left even my parents and sister I loved so much for dead. To me, everyone but me is 'just someone else.' I couldn't care less if they live or die, so…what meaning is there in me making relationships with anyone? I'm sure that in the end I will betray them."

From Yumiko's presence, her gaze, and her breathing, Minoru could tell that she felt pity for him. It made him only look down farther as he hugged his knees and muttered, "That's… enough. I could never be as strong as you. In this world, I cannot believe that there would be anyone whom I don't feel is an outsider."

"You're probably right," Yumiko said in the cold air of the parking garage, her voice slightly shaking. "I could never like someone like you, to be honest."

But as Minoru curled up even tighter, Yumiko put her hands on his shoulders and gripped tightly. "Even so, I'll believe in you. I'll believe in the you who came running to save me from Biter," she said.

Just as she finished talking, the rumble of the elevator overlapped her voice.

Suddenly, a soft feeling and sweet scent wrapped around Minoru.

By the time Minoru realized he had been embraced, Yumiko had already started walking toward the black minivan.

It was midnight on Tuesday, December 17.

The minivan, driven by DD, headed north from SFD Headquarters in East Shinjuku and got onto the expressway at the Gokokuji interchange. They cut southeast across the center of Tokyo and headed down the Fukagawa line at the Hakozaki Junction. At the Tatsumi Junction they entered the Wangan line and got off at Ariake.

Ariake Heaven's Shore was a large water park located to the west of the Yurikamome line's Ariake Tennis-no-Mori Station. Its selling point apparently was that the entire facility was indoors, and even in the winter people could wear swimsuits and feel like they were at a tropical resort.

Minoru, of course, had not seen nor been there himself.

After exiting the expressway, they took a right at the first intersection and after driving straight for a little while saw the silhouette of the building.

Minoru had memorized the layout of the building during

the pre-mission meeting, but after seeing the real thing, he thought that it was huge. The floor plan had an area of two hundred by three hundred meters, which, according to Olivier, was nearly as big as the entire east exhibition building of Tokyo Big Sight. That didn't really help Minoru much, though. Anyway, they were going to have to locate one man covertly, somewhere within the entirety of this giant water park.

Currently, Professor Riri, who had hacked into the security camera network at the park, was trying to track down Igniter based on the footage, but they had not received word from her yet.

"Wouldn't it be faster for us to just use our powers in the middle of the park and lure him out with our scent?" said Olivier from the front passenger's seat as he held on to a long rodlike case, but DD shook his head.

"Igniter isn't someone who'd fall for a clear trap like that. Plus, he's got a national certification, so he's probably one of the more intelligent Ruby Eyes we've ever fought."

"Well, I suppose so, being an ex–company president and all," replied Olivier as he made a "hmph" sound, just as the minivan started to slow down and stopped on the side of the road.

According to the car navigation system it was 12:50 a.m. There were still a lot of open lots in the surrounding area, so once the engine was cut, it was so quiet a person wouldn't think they were in the middle of Tokyo.

Behind a fence on the right that extended on and on in either direction, there was a building with an elliptical dome. It looked like the clear tube that came out of the roof might be a waterslide. It was probably really busy during the day, but now it was as quiet as an old ruin.

Suddenly, a clear voice rang out over the miniature intercom attached to Minoru's left ear.

"I see you've made it there," Riri said. "I'm sorry, but I still haven't been able to locate Igniter. However, I do know that he is currently there working. Please wait a little longer in the van on standby."

"Gotcha," replied DD. "...Hm?"

DD suddenly leaned forward.

"Wait a minute, I think... It's really, really faint, but I think I can smell him."

Tension ran high through the minivan. Riri's voice also grew sharper.

"You sensed Igniter? Does that mean that he is using his power at this very moment?" Riri asked.

"No... The scent is way too faint for that... I'm sorry, I can't tell exactly where he is. I do think he is in the southwest area of the building, though...," DD replied.

"All right... I'll focus my search using the cameras in that area. Wait a minute."

A strained silence went on for more than thirty seconds.

"...I found him! There's no mistaking it. It's definitely Igniter. But...what on earth is he doing...?" Riri said with suspicion in her voice, but she quickly changed her tone and snapped out orders.

"Let's get him before he has a chance to change position. Do you hear me? His current location is in the center of an area called Coco Island. Since there is no proper entrance nearby, we'll have Oli-V make a cut in the outer wall. Approach him from all directions and surround him on all sides!"

"Gotcha!"

"Roger!"

"Got it!"

DD, Olivier, and Yumiko all answered in sharp tones, but Minoru was just barely able to squeeze out a "G-got it."

Feeling with his left hand, Minoru made sure he had his air canister securely in his school uniform pocket. Minoru still wasn't sure whether his defensive shell would cut off the effective range of Igniter's power. However, Minoru probably would never have the chance to test whether or not that was true. As soon as they got a visual confirmation on the enemy, Yumiko would dash forward and disable him with either her stun baton or knife.

There's probably nothing that I'll need to do this time, so there's no reason for me to be scared, Minoru thought to himself and followed Yumiko out of the van.

After climbing over the blue-painted fence, they found themselves in a large parking lot. There were white lines drawn out as far as the eye could see, but of course right now there were hardly any parked cars.

DD took in another deep breath of air, pointed in one direction, and started running. DD, who was of small build and wearing his camouflage vest over a black tracksuit, ran silently and with hardly any swaying motion, so much that he looked like he belonged in a ninja movie.

Olivier followed in his blazer uniform with that rodlike case over his shoulder, and Yumiko, also in her uniform, ran beside him. At the end of the line, Minoru dashed along as silently as he possibly could, trying to keep up.

In less than ten seconds they cut across the parking lot and stood up against the exterior wall of the giant dome building.

Checking the map with his smartphone, DD pointed beyond the wall.

"Our destination, Coco Island, is about thirty meters behind this wall, let's enter from here."

Even though DD said "from here," all Minoru could see in front of him was a thick concrete wall. As Minoru tilted his head in confusion, Olivier replied, "Got it, boss," with no trace of nervousness in his voice and stepped forward.

Olivier unzipped the zipper on his rodlike case and stuck

his hand inside. Upon seeing something very different from a fishing pole come out, Minoru opened his eyes wide.

It was a sword.

To top it off, it wasn't a wooden sword or a Japanese sword, either. It had a black sheath decorated with silver, as well as a silver-colored hilt. It perfectly fit the description of a western long sword.

Beside Minoru, who was dumbfounded, Yumiko looked shocked and whispered, "Where the hell did you buy something like that?"

"Last time when we were sent to Kamakura I stopped by a weapons shop, you see," said Olivier, the half-Japanese, half-French pretty boy grinning as he took the hilt of the sword in his right hand.

Shinng! went the vigorous sound of the sword as he unsheathed it, and the blade shined silver like a mirror. It was clear that it was the real thing.

"Be more quiet when you take it out!!" DD yelled.

"But the sound is one of the best parts!!" Olivier argued.

After arguing back and forth a little while, Olivier lifted up the heavy-looking sword with his right hand as if it weighed nothing and then... *Fyu-fyu!* went the sound of the rushing air as Olivier swung the sword so fast one couldn't follow it with their eyes. With another ringing sound, he resheathed the sword and turned back around.

No matter how closely Minoru looked at the wall, he couldn't see a single scratch on it. However, when DD took out a suction cup from his waist pouch and attached it to the wall and pulled, an eighteen-centimeter-square section of the wall came out.

Minoru gulped when he saw the smoothness of the edge of the cut. The thickness of the wall was more than twenty inches, including the concrete outer wall, insulation, and the inner wall. To top it off, there were also thick steel beams running from bottom to top and left to right, and yet the cut was glossy and smooth as if it were polished.

"Ah!" Minoru suddenly remembered that he had felt the same astonishment the previous Friday, when he saw Biter's tooth in that glass petri dish. As soon as Professor Riri pushed on it with tweezers, it split in two halves, showing edges polished like mirrors.

Professor Riri had said that the tooth was cut using the power of one of the SFD members. Manipulating the van der Waals forces between particles, they were able to cut surfaces so that they were extremely smooth. The code name of that member was...

"So...Oli-V is 'Divider'?" Minoru muttered, and with a twinkling in his eye, the bespectacled pretty boy struck a pose.

"...Again have I cut down something worthle—"

"That's enough of that," interrupted Yumiko, hitting Olivier in the side, so that he grimaced and got quiet.

DD gently placed the concrete block on the ground and removed the suction cup, placing it back in his side pouch.

"All right, then. From here on out, anyone who uses their power is going to have Igniter's attention drawn to them. We will approach him without using our powers, surround him, and then attack while he's off his guard. We'll leave the first strike to Yumiko. As for backup...we're counting on you, Isolator."

"...What?" Minoru's heart thumped loudly in his chest.

Olivier glanced at Minoru from the corner of his eye and said, "My power doesn't match well with Igniter's. After all, I can't cut oxygen. Your shell'll be a lot more effective, right?"

Olivier, the long-sword user, then stepped over to Minoru and put his left arm around Minoru's neck and whispered, "If you're still bothered about me smacking you, then come on and show us some courage, man."

It's not a matter of me showing or not showing courage or determination. I don't have any to begin with, Minoru muttered to himself inside his head.

Yumiko then grabbed Olivier by his uniform and pulled him away from Minoru.

"What are you doing giving him unnecessary pressure? I'll take care of Igniter in one hit, so I won't be needing any backup. He's my prey," Yumiko said in a low voice, before crouching down and stepping through the square hole in the wall.

Following DD and Olivier, Minoru also slipped through the hole and into the water park, taking care not to catch the sharp edge on his clothing.

Green emergency lamps shined their light on a cramped walkway that continued left and right in a gentle curve. It seemed to be a passageway for employees, and piping could be seen on the walls and ceiling.

DD ran left without saying a word. After Minoru ran a few steps after him, he heard Professor Riri's voice over the intercom in his left ear.

"...I have confirmed your entrance from here. Igniter still hasn't moved from the Coco Island area. If you continue down the passageway and take the fourth flight of stairs on your left, you will enter the attraction area. ...All right, I have a message from the other team. Listen as you go."

Other team? thought Minoru, and a moment later after a short break of noise, he heard a voice he had never heard before in his left ear.

"This is Refractor speaking. I have successfully infiltrated Ignite's, aka Ayato Suka's, apartment."

The voice was a girl's voice, with a low and calm tone, but it still contained a bit of youthfulness to it. Minoru hadn't heard her code name before. She must be a Jet Eye who Minoru hadn't been introduced to yet, but still...

"Are you all right...doing something like infiltrating Igniter's apartment?" Minoru asked.

What if Igniter had cameras set up in his apartment and was checking those cameras remotely? Minoru thought, worried, but Yumiko who was running beside him gave him a short answer.

"It's all right, you can't see her."

Can't...see her?

Refract... The meaning of that word was, if Minoru remembered correctly..."to bend light."

The girl's voice continued. "The rooms are filled with ornamental plants, as well as a large aquarium... That too is filled with plants; there are no fish."

"Plants, huh...?" Riri's voice joined in over the transmission. "I see. Is there anything else you notice?"

"There is hardly any furniture... There isn't a television or computer, either. Ah! On the living room wall there is a large map."

"A map?"

"A map of the metropolitan area. There are lots of pushpins pushed in on the map."

Minoru and the other three kept running and listening without saying a word. Doors and flights of stairs rushed past them as they ran.

"There are nine pins marking places on the map, and seven pins in the margins."

"Tell me the locations of some of those pins," said Riri.

"West Arai in the Adachi district, the west exit of Ikebukuro Station, West Shinjuku 1-chome."

Minoru could tell over the intercom that Riri took a deep breath.

"So all of the locations where he has committed crimes up until now."

"Wait. There are some places that are marked even where

there aren't any pins. If you connect the dots…it forms a large ellipse. A zero…? Or maybe an *O*?"

"An *O*? If the pins are… Nine plus seven makes sixteen, so sixteen *O*… That's oxygen's elementary number! So this is Igniter's plan! He plans to leave this signature in the middle of Tokyo!!"

Clang! went the sound of a chair getting knocked back as Riri's rushed voice came over the intercom.

"Tell me all of the places where there aren't pins placed yet!"

"All right, most of the pins are to the north, and most of the marks are to the south. Jingu-mae in the Shibuya district… Kaki-no-ki-zaka in the Meguro district… Ariake in the Koto district…"

"There is a mark on Kaki-no-ki-zaka in the Meguro district? That's where Yousuke Nakakubo's residence is… There's no pin there?"

"Correct. There's only a marker there."

"What does this mean? We already found a dead body there."

In the back of his mind, Minoru could not help but think back to the scene in the basement of Nakakubo's home, that flooded wine cellar and its floating corpse.

At that moment, Minoru remembered the anxiety he had felt earlier, that there was a disconnect in their understanding of Igniter, and twisted his face in thought.

Something is off. Something is wrong, he thought. But before he could find a proper reason for that feeling, DD, who had been running ahead, stopped.

DD pointed to the left with his finger. The dark entrance to the fourth flight of stairs opened up out of the concrete wall. Igniter was just ahead. DD motioned with his hands that first he would enter, followed by Olivier, Yumiko, and then finally Minoru. They would surround him from all sides and attack.

This was not the time to be thinking about unnecessary things. Minoru nodded along with Yumiko and Olivier. DD, in his black tracksuit, then soundlessly disappeared into the darkness, followed by Yumiko and Olivier in their blazer uniforms.

After checking the hose from the air canister that extended up to his collar, Minoru took a deep breath and silently raced up the narrow staircase.

After about twenty steps, there was a stainless steel door. DD, who was up against it, sniffed and nodded. Then, he carefully turned the silver knob.

The door opened with a quiet *click*.

From the crack in the door, a dark orange-colored light shone in, and with it came the smell of cool, damp air. In that air was not only the smell of water, but also a sort of chemical smell.

What is that smell...? Minoru thought, as DD disappeared on the other side of the door. Olivier with his sword and Yumiko with her stun baton followed after him.

Wiping his sweaty hands on his uniform, Minoru went up the last step and through the door. What he saw was a section of tiles made to look like light brown bricks and several palm trees beyond it. Between the hairy trunks of the palm trees an orange light waved back and forth.

It wasn't fire, just reflections from the lighting... In other words, water, and that chemical smell was the smell of chlorine.

It was a pool.

That made sense, as Ariake Heaven's Shore was a water theme park with the goal of making one feel like they were at a tropical resort even during the winter, but...

At that instant, Minoru finally reached the source of the disconnect he was feeling.

Why was the wine cellar flooded?

Why was the real Ayato Suka, who had defrauded Igniter's company out of a large amount of money, not incinerated?

Why did Nakakubo's residence in Kaki-no-ki-zaka in Meguro have a mark for a future incident, but not a pin for an already completed crime?

The answer was that that place was still being prepared. He still planned on burning the real Suka. The water that filled the basement was part of that preparation. The water wasn't there to slow the discovery of the corpse.

Water's chemical formula was H_2O. In other words, it was composed of one-third oxygen.

That water was his fuel.

"Professor! Professor!!" Minoru whispered loudly into the intercom.

"What is it? DD and the others have already surrounded the pool! Hurry up, Mikkun!"

"No...this is a trap! The true nature of Igniter's power is not fire, it's water!!"

"W-water, you say?" Riri replied in a strained voice.

"Exactly. Nakakubo... Igniter was infected by his Third Eye moments from drowning. If the source of Igniter's power comes from his fear of death, then it must also come from a fear of water. Igniter's power to control oxygen is fundamentally the power to separate water into hydrogen and oxygen!!"

An instant of silence.

"Oxyhydrogen... In other words, explosive hydrogen knallgas!!" Riri shouted.

The principles Minoru had learned in middle school chemistry flashed in the back of his mind.

When oxygen and hydrogen gases were combined in a 1:2 ratio and ignited, they would instantly and violently react, giving off high heat and a shock wave. In other words, they would explode. That mixture of gases was called oxyhydrogen, or hydrogen knallgas.

In order to make the explosive gas, one would only have to prepare tanks of pure oxygen and pure hydrogen and open them both at the same time. However, by this method, it was difficult to get an exact ratio of 1:2. However, there was a simpler method that gave a much more accurate ratio of the gases, and that was to separate water through electrification. Water's chemical formula was H_2O, so when it was separated, for every O_2 molecule created, there would be two H_2 molecules created. A perfect ratio of 1:2.

"Mikkun," said Riri in despair. "It's too late. Yukko's about to rush in."

* * *

A fatal poison and life's miracle medicine.

Yousuke Nakakubo stood still in the center of a one-meter-deep pool, still wearing his work clothes, touching the surface of the water with his right hand.

Deep in the mountains of Okutama, he had stood like this every day in the middle of a stream and resonated with the high concentration of oxygen there.

Compared to the oxygen molecules floating about in the atmosphere, the oxygen tied to H_2O molecules was both incredibly stubborn and proud. Even if Nakakubo tried to grasp them, his five fingers would not budge, as if he had gripped a clump of steel. They would reject the control of his Third Eye.

However, in these past few days, Nakakubo's power had made several far-reaching advancements. He could already grasp half of the oxygen in his aquarium at his apartment at once. In other words, he could separate water into oxygen and hydrogen. At this rate, soon he would be able to grasp all of the oxygen in the water that filled his wine cellar, ignite the resulting oxyhydrogen, and blast away not only Ayato Suka's corpse, but also his entire residence in Meguro that the thieving banks had stolen from him like hyenas.

After that, he would continue to grasp larger amounts of water, drawing a ^{16}O oxygen symbol in the center of the city, and finally he would blow away the entire Ariake Heaven's Shore water park with its pools.

Plus, he would do it during operating hours. He would cleanse all those writhing foolish humans all at once.

If he could get that far, it would be no exaggeration to say that all fourteen million souls in Tokyo would be in his hands. Every river and pond, every water tank atop a building, and all of the water piped throughout the city would serve him as a high-purity explosive.

He would blow them all away, together with all of human civilization.

"...Heh, heh-heh, heh-heh-heh," Nakakubo laughed, and small waves spread out from his right hand across the surface of the water.

But just then...

Throb! ...The sphere in his right hand pulsed.

The pain left as quickly as it had come, but Nakakubo held his breath, opened his eyes wide, and used all of his five senses to search the surroundings of the pool.

Nakakubo couldn't sense the organic solvent-like smell of the black hunters. He couldn't see anything moving, and he couldn't hear any footsteps. Furthermore, it was just too soon. He had only just been approached by them nine hours ago. For them to find Nakakubo's real name from seeing his face, to search his old residence in Meguro, to find the body, to see through his disguise as Ayato Suka and trace that to Ariake Heaven's Shore... Nakakubo didn't believe that they could accomplish something like that in half a day.

However, at the same time in the back of his mind he heard the words of that woman from the organization, Liquidizer.

"The black ones have already started to move."

Impossible, thought Nakakubo in denial. *It would be impossible for them to track me down this fast.* But the throbbing of his right hand just moments ago couldn't have just been inside his head.

It must have been a warning from the oxygen in the air around him. The possibility that he was already surrounded was high.

Nakakubo looked left and right again.

Coco Island was, as its name inferred, an attraction based off the image of a southern island's beach with coconut palms. The large circular pool was surrounded by a man-made beach, and around it real palms were planted.

During the park's hours, sunlight poured in from the glass dome roof, but now it was lit by only the orange color of its reserve lighting. The area beyond the palm trees was completely shrouded in darkness, and even with his strengthened vision, it was hard to see through it.

If his enemies were hiding in that darkness, Nakakubo, who was standing in the middle of the pool with water up to his stomach, would have been seen by them long ago. If he was suddenly rushed, he wouldn't have the time to stage an oxygen-deprivation attack, and he wouldn't be able to deal with multiple enemies at a time with his combustion attack.

If that was the case, then…

He didn't have any other options.

Here, Nakakubo would use the true power hidden in his right hand, his explosive oxyhydrogen attack, to blow away all of the surrounding black hunters at once. If he dived to the bottom of the pool, he should be able to avoid the brunt of the attack.

The problem was how to ignite it. No matter how much oxyhydrogen he was able to generate, if there was not a spark, he

couldn't make it explode. Is there anything he could use? he thought. He didn't need a flame, if he could just cause a small spark, that would be enough...

But then Nakakubo's lips moved and twisted into a smile. His left hand moved into a pocket of his work clothes and grabbed onto something.

* * *

Even if Minoru screamed out a warning, he wouldn't make it in time.

He didn't know how much oxyhydrogen Igniter would be able to generate, but the shock wave of its explosion would be faster than sound. No matter how fast Accelerator Yumiko was, there was no way that she would be able to escape unscathed.

Minoru could only think of one other way to save Yumiko from the impending explosion.

This isn't a matter of can or cannot do, Minoru thought. *I'll do it. I will do this.*

Minoru clenched his teeth, stood up, and then ran forward toward the pool as fast as he could.

* * *

Here they come!! Nakakubo thought, feeling the movement of oxygen molecules before he could even see them.

From between the palms on the north side of the pool, about thirty meters away, a black shadow came flying toward him at an incredible speed. Her long hair flowed behind her as she came out of the faint darkness. He could see a fluttering skirt, a stun baton in her right hand, and a knife in her left.

It was his mortal enemy, that Accelerator girl.

The fact that the ground at his enemy's feet was sand worked to Nakakubo's advantage. In order to create sufficient acceleration to work off of, the girl had taken several steps in the sand without using her power.

Not wanting to waste the extra two seconds of time given to him, Nakakubo took his company cell phone out of his pocket, crushed it in his left hand, and threw it as hard as he could toward her.

In the air, the lithium battery, which had shorted, let out a white flame.

At the exact same moment...

Nakakubo extended his right hand toward the water's surface in front of her, and...

He howled.

"Oooooooxygeeeeeeeennnn!!!! Ahhh!!!!"

The eye in his hand opened wide and let out a crimson beam of light.

It was so hard!

The bones in his hand creaked and his tendons stretched.

The muscles in the back of his hand leaped up abnormally and split his skin, spraying a mist of blood.

Oxygen.

Molecules of oxygen! Heed my call! Purify!

"Aaaahhhh!"

The pain was so much that he felt dizzy, and a splintered tip of bone shot out from his right hand.

But finally Nakakubo grasped it and clenched his hand into a fist.

A red light shone brilliantly through the blood of his hand, and then...

Pssh! The sharp sound of an impact shook the air, and the surface of the water instantly vaporized. A hemisphere of water ten meters in diameter was gone.

The air wavered like a mirage where the water had been.

In the space of air that girl was just about to charge through, a large quanity of oxygen and hydrogen molecules were separated, waiting for the time for them to reunite.

In other words, for combustion.

In all of nature this was the most beautiful, simplest, and most dangerous kind of combustion.

A shiver of electric excitement raced up Nakakubo's spine. Raising his broken right hand high into the air, Nakakubo fell backward into the water...

...just as his cell phone, showering sparks, made contact with the explosive oxyhydrogen gas.

＊ ＊ ＊

Minoru ran.

He knew that he was running, but he could hardly feel himself kicking the ground beneath his feet. However, he raced forward at an incredible speed and saw Yumiko's silhouette dash forward toward him from his right.

Bursting through the palm trees and across the beach, in just three meters he would come into contact with Yumiko.

But just then, the water's surface to his left disappeared with a strange rumbling sound.

Igniter had separated the water molecules. At the same time, something engulfed in white flames came flying toward him.

He didn't have a second before the gas ignited and exploded.

There was only one way to protect Yumiko now.

It was not enough to activate his defensive shield and stand in front of her. Yumiko had already rushed into the explosive oxyhydrogen air. Even if Minoru became a shield for her, the heat and shock wave would easily destroy Yumiko's body.

He couldn't just cover her...

He had to take her into his defensive shell.

The shell activated by the Third Eye in Minoru's chest

materialized about three centimeters away from him, and in that instant everything on that boundary that Minoru rejected as a foreign substance would be ejected from his shell.

No matter how small Yumiko was, there was no possible way she could fit in that space of three centimeters. So normally one would expect Yumiko to be ejected. At least, that's what would happen if Minoru considered her a "foreign substance."

If it was a random person on the street, that's exactly what would happen.

Only eleven days had passed since Minoru had met Yumiko in Akigase Park.

In the back of Minoru's mind, the times Minoru saw Yumiko flashed before his eyes.

Yumiko, her eyes flashing as she stormed over to Minoru. Yumiko, her mouth stuffed with spaghetti. Yumiko, looking down beside Sanae. Yumiko, staring at the scars on her leg.

And Yumiko after she had saved Minoru's life, her back turned to him, crying.

At that moment he finally thought of the sheer magnitude of the pain and suffering she held in her chest.

He couldn't let her die here.

He didn't want her to die.

One day he wanted to see her true smile, after she had overcome all her painful memories.

This is not for me, Minoru thought. *This is not simply because I don't want to increase the number of painful memories I have. ...I want to protect her!*

"*Yumiko!*" Minoru shouted.

Minoru's vision to his left had gone pure white.

In that instant Minoru wrapped both arms around Yumiko and held her tightly, activating his defensive shell.

A suddenly expanding light engulfed them both, and the world melted away. In the scene devoid of color and sound,

Minoru saw two black shadows rotating as they were sent flying. It was Yumiko's stun baton and knife.

But those were the only two things that were sent away. Even with his shell fully activated, the warmth and presence of Yumiko did not disappear from his two arms.

At that moment the enormous quantity of hydrogen and oxygen molecules fused back together.

Because they were insulated from the shock wave and the sound was cut off, to Minoru it looked like a scene from a silent movie. The white sand at Minoru's feet was instantly blown away and the rows of palm trees were knocked down.

The supersonic shock wave broke all the glass dividing walls surrounding the pool, and after colliding with the concrete walls, it shot upward. The light metal frame and panes of glass could not withstand the pressure, expanded, and shattered into pieces. As the glass shards floated in the water vapor resulting from the explosion, Minoru took his eyes away from the destructive phenomenon and turned to look at Yumiko in his arms.

The black-haired girl stared up at Minoru, with her eyes wide, as if she hadn't looked at the explosion in the first place.

In those eyes, large tears suddenly formed, and her lips quivered as if she was trying to say something.

* * *

Even after escaping under one meter or so of water, Nakakubo still couldn't escape the roaring sound of the explosion.

He felt a shock as if he had been hit by a hammer, and both of his ears went numb. His broken right hand was also filled with an intense pain, but compared to the storm of exhilaration filling his entire body, it was nothing.

The sheer amount of force he unleashed with just one grip!

He had finally awoken to his true power.

It was frustrating that he had been cornered by the black hunters, but given this outcome he could even count it as a plus, as he was able to reach the stage of becoming "Purifier" far earlier than he had expected.

Now not only air, but water was subject to his will.

Just you watch, Nakakubo thought. *You fools, you who have continued to waste oxygen in pursuit of profits unhinged from reality. I'll teach you how humanity is nothing but a bane to this world.*

As the explosion wound down, the surface of the water got closer to him. Water from the surrounding area was flowing into the gap of the water he had separated earlier.

Nakakubo put his left hand on the bottom of the pool for support and slowly stood up out of the water.

That Accelerator girl should have been blown away without a trace, but her companions behind her might still be alive. He still had to finish them off with an oxygen-deprivation attack, he thought, and turned his gaze to the thick clouds of water vapor floating in the air.

But shocked, after seeing something he could not believe, he groaned.

* * *

Just as something was about to be said from Yumiko's lips, Minoru saw movement out of the corner of his eye to the left and immediately transferred his attention to it.

Beyond the steam from the explosion, that man was standing.

Yousuke Nakakubo—Igniter. The Ruby Eye with the power to manipulate oxygen. His thin face and teacher-like intellectual air... There was no mistaking that this was the man Minoru had seen in Ikebukuro. His face showed his age, but he did not at all look decrepit or infirm. As if projecting the swirling emotions within him, both of his eyes glinted with a harsh light.

The emotions expressed in his eyes went from shock then anger to rage and the intent to kill. His lips twisted, and he seemed to shout something, but Minoru could not hear him.

Holding up his wounded right hand, the crimson sphere embedded in the center of his palm overflowed with a dazzling light.

* * *

How?

How were they still alive?

That boy carrying that girl in his stiff-collared school uniform..., Nakakubo thought. *This is the first time I have seen his face, but I remember his presence. It's the same one who was riding on the back of that motorcycle in Ikebukuro.* No matter where he looked he couldn't find a single scratch on either of them.

Nakakubo's shock immediately lit up and burned in an incredible rage.

How dare they reject the Purifier's flames...

"Don't think you can get away with this!!" he screamed, throwing his broken right hand out toward them.

Ignoring the pain, he clenched his fingers and pulled all the oxygen away from the black hunters. A wind picked up and blew away the steam.

Those two who should have had the oxygen needed to breathe taken away from them, they should have immediately collapsed into the water.

However...

".......Why?" Nakakubo groaned.

The girl and boy stood still in the wave-tossed water, without moving an inch. Their expressions didn't even change. The light in all four of their eyes did not waver one bit.

"Why?!?!" he screamed again and tried to grip his right hand together with all his might.

But before his five fingers were able to grasp it, an intense feeling of resistance ran up his entire right arm.

It was too hard, he couldn't grasp it.

It was an absolute rejection unlike any he had felt before. A thin layer of air surrounding the two black hunters was completely out of his control.

"Ahh!! Aaahh!!!!" No matter how he yelled, no matter how much force he put into it, he could not close his right hand.

This was impossible. Absolutely impossible.

All oxygen in existence was on Nakakubo's side. At his will they would move, split, combine, and lay down judgment on humans, and yet...

Within the burning anger racing through his veins, Nakakubo felt a slight, barely there chill spreading inside him.

"Is this...fear?" he thought.

At that moment the boy took one step forward.

✳ ✳ ✳

The stun baton and knife had both flown off somewhere, but Minoru knew that they were no longer needed. All he needed to do was take a step and kick off from the ground.

"...Accelerate me," Minoru whispered, and Yumiko in his arms gave a vigorous nod.

With his right foot, Minoru kicked off from the bare concrete freed of its sand by the explosion.

Yumiko took Minoru's step and accelerated it.

While still wrapped in Minoru's invisible defensive shell, Minoru and Yumiko shot forward at an incredible speed. The water's surface at Minoru's feet parted left and right and shot up in tall walls on either side of them.

The more than thirty meters between them and Igniter went to zero in an instant, and Minoru's left shoulder collided with Igniter's thin chest.

Minoru hardly felt any recoil, but even across his shell Minoru could feel the old man's ribs and sternum break. From the Ruby Eye's wide-opened mouth came trails of blood, and after being thrown backward, he landed in the sand a great distance away.

Of the body's four limbs, Igniter's right hand alone rose unsteadily upward, as if it had a mind of its own. But after a short while its light faded, disappeared, and his right hand fell back into the sand.

Igniter didn't try to move after that, and it didn't appear that his Third Eye would go berserk.

Minoru let out the breath of air he had been holding in and deactivated his shell. Upon which the warm surrounding water rushed in and swallowed his lower body.

"Wha—! Hey! If you're going to deactivate your shell, wait until we're out of the pool!" Yumiko cried out, flustered, in Minoru's ear.

"Oh... I-I'm sorry," Minoru replied, finally realizing that he still had his arms wrapped around Yumiko's back.

Whoa! thought Minoru, but instead of heeding his intention of letting Yumiko go, his arms just wrapped around her more tightly.

"..." Minoru heard Yumiko taking a deep breath, but she didn't try to push him away.

There was a short silence.

"...I'm so glad you're all right...," Minoru said, his voice shaking. "...If you had been thrown out of my shell and only I was unharmed...I just don't know what I would have done."

"...Huh? You mean... You weren't sure that wouldn't happen?"

"N-no... I thought that it might have been about fifty-fifty...?"

"Are you serious?!" This time, Yumiko put her hands on Minoru's chest and pushed him away, glaring at him from up close. "Let's say that you activated your shell while hugging me and I was rejected. Wouldn't all of the bones in my body have cracked and broken?"

"...That's a good point."

"Geez...," Yumiko muttered, pursing her lips, before shrugging and—while about 30 percent of it was wry—giving Minoru a smile.

She wrapped her arms around Minoru's back again and hugged him as tightly as she could. With their noses almost touching, she added in a short whisper from her glossy lips, "But still... Thank you."

As they continued to embrace in the water, Minoru thought it strange that he felt he wanted to stay like this forever. In the future, a time might come when he would want to forget this memory as well. But Minoru hoped from the bottom of his heart that that would not happen.

Yumiko's eyes, bordered by long eyelashes, reflected the light coming up from the surface of the water and shined. Minoru could see her white teeth like pearls from behind her slightly opened lips.

Just then.

"Hey now, just how long do you plan on staying like that, you lovebirds?"

As soon as that voice rang out, *boom!* The air shook as Minoru's arms suddenly went empty. Yumiko had accelerated herself as she jumped away.

Yumiko landed on a sandy beach a long distance away from Minoru, who had frozen in a bit of a stupid-looking pose, and with her face bright red she pointed past the row of palm trees.

"What are you two doing, peeking at us?! I'm going to blow you away!"

"Talk about mean, we actually had to deal with that giant explosion, you know?" said Olivier Saito as he walked out from behind the line of palm trees shaking his head, leaves stuck in his curly hair. DD followed behind him, smirking.

Both of them had been hidden behind Igniter, and even though they didn't look like they had sustained a lot of damage, they should have been hit by the shock wave. Olivier's long sword was unsheathed in his right hand, so he must have done something about it with his power.

DD, who looked on for a while as Yumiko went around chasing Olivier as he fled, walked over to Igniter, who hadn't moved since he collapsed.

After putting his hand on Igniter's neck to check his pulse, he took a syringe from his waist pouch and quickly administered some kind of drug.

Minoru, who waded through the water out of the pool, asked in a small voice, "Is...he still alive?"

"Yeah. A Third Eye host isn't going to die from just an external shock like that," DD replied. "You would need to completely destroy their heart or brain...or you could cut off their supply of oxygen. In that sense, this guy really was a 'Third Eye killer.' We're lucky to have you on our side, Utsugi."

"I-it's nothing like that, all I did was...," Minoru started.

"Don't be modest, Mikkun," said Professor Riri suddenly over the intercom. "You played a vital part in everything from confirming the enemy's identity and seeing through his power to the actual battle. You have done well. No longer does anyone in the SFD doubt your power or your determination."

After hearing that, Minoru reflexively looked at Olivier.

Divider Olivier, who seemed to have been listening to the same transmission, smiled with his pretty face and let out a big laugh before giving Minoru a thumbs-up with his right hand. His beautiful voice rang out over the destroyed pool with a volume level rivaling an oncoming siren.

"Good job!"

DD and Yumiko both shook their heads at the same time.

12

"...kubo. Mr. Nakakubo."

His shoulder shaken, the man opened his eyes.

"If you sleep here, you'll catch a cold."

The voice was that of a young nurse wearing a white frock. The man, after giving a short answer, lightly shook his head back and forth. He felt as if he had been having a long strange dream, but he couldn't remember what had happened in it.

As he watched the nurse smile and walk away, the man readjusted himself on the hard sofa.

The hospital's lounge area was, as always, wrapped in a heavy, sluggish sort of atmosphere. The smell of snacks and the heater turned up too high was enough to make it difficult to breathe, but the man really didn't have anywhere else he could go.

On a large flat-screen television that was hung from the ceiling, commentators on a variety show were talking in raised voices.

"...It had to be a terrorist attack! A new kind of terrorist attack! There's no way that could have been an accident. I mean, how does a pool just explode?!"

"But they couldn't find any traces of explosives, right? Wasn't it just some sort of gas leak?"

"That's why I said before, do you think they're really running gas pipes under a pool?!"

Then, an aerial photograph of a large dome-shaped building with its roof blown off was displayed on the screen.

It was the same news that Nakakubo had gotten bored of watching over the past week. In the first place, he couldn't care less if a theme park exploded or fell apart. It wasn't like it was a place that he would ever visit anyway.

After all, he had dragged his family into a murder-suicide and yet brazenly survived himself.

Nakakubo shook his head and let out a deep sigh, then grimaced from the pain of his fractured ribs.

He couldn't at all remember what he had done in the three months between the time he had driven his car off of Ooi Pier and was admitted to the hospital.

Given the fact that he had been found with five of his ribs and sternum broken, not to mention the hideous state of his right hand, it was clear that he had gotten wrapped up in some sort of incident, but no matter how he thought about it, he didn't feel that those memories would ever return to him and had already given up on it.

With another sigh, the man stood up and walked over to the glass-enclosed smoking area in the corner of the lounge. He took a lighter and a pack of cigarettes from his pocket and lit up.

After taking a deep breath of smoke, he felt a prickling sensation at the back of his throat. It was as if he had abstained from cigarettes during those three months he had forgotten, but that was impossible. Before he attempted suicide, he had smoked two packs a day.

Letting out a long puff of smoke, Nakakubo looked at his right hand holding his cigarette.

It looked terrible. Most of his hand was in a cast, and he could only move the tips of his fingers. He couldn't see it now, but there was also a strange wound in the center of his hand.

There was a circular depression, as if someone had scooped out the middle of his palm with a spoon. The doctor said that he must have hit it against a sharp object, but the wound didn't go through to the back of his hand.

Apart from that...

As he looked at that wound, Nakakubo felt a strange sense of loss. He felt far more lonely than he felt toward the loss of his fashion-crazed wife and unemployed middle-age son. He felt as if he had lost something truly important.

"Hmph," he said with a wry smile and took his eyes away from his cast-wrapped hand. He looked up at the ceiling and let out a long, narrow stream of smoke.

Suddenly, in the back of his mind, a melody popped up, and subconsciously with his raspy voice he began to hum.

"Hmm-hmhm, hmmm-hmmhmm..."

He couldn't remember any lyrics, but he still hummed the melody ceaselessly, tirelessly.

Hmm...hmmhm...

The smoke, which was separated by the beats in the rhythm, twisted into a strange form as it rose before it was sucked up into the filter of the air purifier.

The End

AFTERWORD

Thank you for reading my first volume of the year, *The Isolator: Realization of Absolute Solitude*, Volume 2!

But really, I can't believe it's already the year 2015... Since my first book was published in February 2009, when this book is published it will be a full six years since my debut. It feels like it all happened in the blink of an eye. At this rate, it won't be long before we get to the year 2019, which is when *Isolator* takes place. I really hope that the consumption tax won't have risen to 12 percent by then!

Next, I'm going to touch on the story, so beware of spoilers from here on out. The "Igniter" arc marks the beginning of when the story really gets set in motion. While the nature of the headquarters and members of the SFD, which Minoru has just joined, has been mostly made clear, there was also a sprinkling of information about the enemy Ruby Eyes' formation. Additionally, near the beginning of the story, the SFD's acting commander, "Professor," explained a little about how the Third Eye's power manipulates objects on an atomic level.

Last year, I went to see the KEK (High Energy Accelerator Research Organization) in Tsukuba City, and really, the more you learn about the world of molecules, atoms, and subatomic particles, the less you understand what anything is anymore! For example, the cover of the book that you are holding right now may be smooth, but if you zoom in to the atomic level, it's a rough grouping of carbon, hydrogen, and metallic atoms, and if you zoom in even more, there are electrons and protons and neutrons that make up the atoms and you can't even pinpoint where they exist at any given time... It's like, what's even going on?

Currently, plans for the construction of the International Linear Collider (ILC), headed by the KEK, are proceeding. It is planned to be the world's largest particle collider, consisting of an underground tunnel thirty kilometers in length, designed to collide electrons and positrons. So in other words, Third Eyes can see, touch, and manipulate a world of particles that you normally would have to go to these great lengths just to observe. If Igniter, who appeared in this volume, had just started a company to generate hydrogen gas from separating water molecules instead of going along with his plans to make Tokyo explode, he probably could have made a lot of money...

Anyway, I've gotten off track. But even so, I think I'd like to continue writing *Isolator* along the lines of a sort of science battle story. Since this author's an "Absolute Liberal Arts" kind of guy, I get the feeling I'll make a couple of mistakes along the way; if you could just send me a message on Twitter or something to correct me, that'd be great!

I want to give my thanks to the illustrator Shimeji, who has drawn all of the new characters full of charm and appeal, and to my editor Miki, who has done a lot to help me draw out the charm and appeal of those characters; you have done a lot for me this volume! I also want to thank you, the reader, and ask for your continued patronage in 2015, this year as well!

A Day in January, 2015
Reki Kawahara